WHITE WEDDING

WHITE WEDDING

KATHLEEN J. WOODS

TUSCALOOSA

FC2 is an imprint of The University of Alabama Press

Inquiries about reproducing material from this work should be addressed
to the University of Alabama Press

Book Design: Publications Unit, Department of English, Illinois State
    University; Director: Steve Halle, Production Assistant: Sarah Urban
Cover design: Lou Robinson
Typeface: Adobe Caslon Pro

Library of Congress Cataloging-in-Publication Data is available from
the Library of Congress.
ISBN: 978-1-57366-192-8
E-ISBN: 978-1-57366-894-1

For Matt

*T*hough the girl had left her some miles away, the woman had seen an invitation. The wedding was easy to find. In the family's house, in the bathroom, she scrubbed her wrists with a soap rose. Blood and cum swirled the sink as the bridal march rang from the backyard. Perfume stung her pores. This late summer morning was hot, growing hotter, the air warmer still in the small, bright room. Sweat brewed under the woman's loose sundress. Thin fabric clung below her breasts, curved with the rise of her mound. She smelled her cunt. She smelled her long night on the road.

She'd left her sandals in Charlotte's car, and the walk had caked her feet further in dirt. She wet a hand towel to scrape her toes. Purple bath mat, purple towel, purple soap in its ivory dish. As she'd slipped through the house, she'd watched caterers sprinkle purple rose petals over white cake. Their quick wrists in starched cuffs, the melon platters and muffin baskets, bouquets of baby's breath and violet roses and banisters dusted in glitter, disposable cameras marked *Use Me (Please)*, an apple crate half-filled with phones. Above, a slideshow tracked the bride and groom through an orchard. The groom was knock-kneed and lanky. The bride was blonde, rosy cheeked, jaw blurred smooth. They held hands and empty fruit baskets. Contrast bleached their white skin. Next, a blank slide with black cursive: *Congratulations, Jordan and Michaela! Photos and Arrangement by Greg.* The projector whirred, pictures looping. The bride peeked out from behind a broad tree trunk. A caterer laid grapes around wilting brie. And on the back lawn, the last welcome guests filled their seats.

Now, the woman straightened in the bathroom mirror, rolling crust from her breastbone, watching her skin inflame and pale. She heard the officiant's greeting. A neighbor's nail gun punctuated his words. *An honor. To have you. Share our joy.* She studied her makeup, the shimmer still on her eyelids, subtle gold. She wiped at smudges of mascara. Returned the hand towel to its towel bar. Appraised the thin, clean cuts on her hands.

Outside the bathroom stretched a long hallway, waxed pine and white doors, narrow light. Family photos crowded the walls. The girl, Charlotte, thin-lipped and wan in class portraits. Michaela, her stepsister, beaming in dance leotards and roller skates, hugging her father in a cap and gown. The woman's shadow rippled through them. She opened a door.

The air inside had been doused in aerosol, a smell like fabric softener, thick and sweet. The woman gagged. But there was a must too, sharp like Charlotte's. She saw the girl's sweatshirt heaped on the cream carpet. There was a white wicker hamper next to a white wicker dresser next to a wrought iron daybed, yellow sheets and a daisy quilt. Across the room, a half-empty bookshelf sat beside a walnut corner desk. A framed ministry license and a computer. A leather chair, clear plastic mat under the wheels.

2

The woman turned back to the dresser. She rifled through the top drawer. Stray socks and underwear. Vinegar sweat. Holes and stains. She searched the dresser's surface—lotion bottles, a saucer of hair ties, a cup of hair sticks and hairpins. A jewelry box, chains tangled and tarnished. She rummaged, then rubbed her teeth with pearl earrings, felt their grit. She slipped the posts through her earlobes. Simple studs. No reason to be greedy here.

The room's single window faced the backyard, thick blinds drawn. A child mumbled a sonnet into a microphone. *Forever* rhymed with *tether*. The woman's brow throbbed. She stretched out over the narrow mattress. Grease lingered on the backs of her arms, clung to the worn quilt. Her temple brushed stiff patches on the pillowcase. Her toes tapped the cool metal frame. Moments passed. She breathed in, smelling scalp and mildew, listening to voices outside and then the steps in the hall. She turned her face toward the opening door.

"Oh. I didn't expect anyone in here." A caterer stood in the doorway, long fingers splayed on the frame. "Should you be in here?"

The woman looked up at the tight vest and purple bow tie and wide cheeks, the ponytail heavy with straight black hair. She saw the other hand tucked against a thigh, clasping shirt cuff to wrist.

"You've caught me dozing."

"We've been asked to keep guests out of the rooms."

"Good. I need to rest before the bride's face needs its touch-up."

The caterer squinted. "You do makeup?"

"And hair." Yawning, she curled onto her side and tilted her head into her hand. "Each and every bridesmaid promised to sob her eyes off before picture time—good, heartfelt tears. All part of the fantasy, right?" She rolled her shoulder. Something cracked. "So here I am, on standby like a sucker." She spoke louder. "Why are you sneaking around?"

Wincing, the caterer glanced down the hall and stepped into the room. She eased the door shut.

"I was hoping to take my break in private."

The woman smiled. "I hope you've smuggled something worth sharing."

Slowly, the caterer smiled back. She shook two nips of gin from her sleeve.

"How did you know?"

"Magic."

They clinked their plastic bottles. They drank.

The caterer shook out her last drops and grimaced. "Do you have a spell for surviving a brunch wedding? Something so I don't throw up in the troughs of scrambled eggs." She clutched her throat. "Soggy eggs. Maybe you can go tell on me. Get me fired."

"I won't tell if you don't." The woman sipped slowly. "If you hate the job, quit."

The caterer sighed. "The job pays. You actually like painting strangers' faces?"

"I only do what I enjoy."

The woman grabbed the caterer's hand and twisted, ignoring the cry as she ran her middle finger straight up the palm.

"Your fate line is weak."

"So I've heard. Look at me, making poor choices all on my own. But—" The caterer winced. "You're squeezing hard."

The woman squeezed harder. The palm was olive beige, pricked with glitter. Her fingertips smelled of garlic and bleach. The woman circled each raised callous. Tickled the aura of

4

veins. As her hand slackened, the caterer sat, warm and heavy. Their bodies crowded the bed.

"I enjoy parts of this job." The caterer tilted away, pulling free. "Just not weddings. Like, everyone's horny and depressed and selfish, and then they start drinking. People are at their absolute worst."

"Open up that last bottle."

Sighing, the caterer produced a third gin. "This is exactly what I mean. What am I doing? This isn't something I do."

A song scraped from the backyard. A cappella. The caterer rolled her eyes, her tear ducts red and clean. The woman watched her swallow. She watched her tongue a stray drop from her lip.

The woman said, "I once watched two guests spend the whole ceremony trying to make the other come. She almost wore enough skirt to hide his hand reaching under it. Really, a little more fabric, and it would have completely covered her hand working his dick. Too bad they started shaking the pew."

The caterer clucked her tongue. "Wow."

"You don't seem especially scandalized."

"I shouldn't be. It's not a wedding without some groping."

"Tell me the worst that you've seen."

"Nothing that wild." She drank and passed the bottle. "Then again, I'm not there for the ceremonies. I've only seen it start up at the cocktail hour—once the appetizers circle, guests start grabbing what they want. But I'm not there to chaperone. It's my job to stand still and describe fillings and pretend I don't see them breathing their spittle all over my tray. I can't say anything about the sauce on their chins or hint that someone else might like a crab cake. And then there are the guests who bend so close I can see every pore and gin blossom, molars packed with quiche, women eating pastry flakes from their bras. They suck the grease off their fingers and it stays on their lips"—she flicked the center button of her vest—"which bloat up, by the way, like everything else. I'm not allowed to say, *hey, slow down, you're making my gums hurt, you're about to pop the zipper on that nice dress, you're hanging out of your shirt*. Nope. It's my job to bring them what they ask for. And I serve the dessert and stand there watching them groan and rub their guts while they shovel cake into their mouths. No, it's not quite a groping, but I swear there have been guests who get off on testing how much food I'll serve them. They'll wave me down, specifically. They'll make a show when I'm stuck standing right there. I once saw a woman do it the whole dinner—feed her husband his plate, then hers. One bite after another, scraping the plates while he turned red and round without saying a word. She called me over to ask for seconds. When she said *please*, she winked. So guess what? I brought them what they asked for." She shivered. "I swear I can still picture them. It makes me want to scream."

The woman leaned close. Their arms touched. "You restrain yourself."

"I keep smiling. I remind myself none of it is real life." She snatched the gin back and drained it, pupils wide.

"And you hide. You do things you don't do." The woman hummed. "They say the thumb holds will. Desire."

"Then what's my thumb after?"

Again, she took up the caterer's hand. "Alas, I don't read palms."

She licked the thumb. Tongued down to its base, the pliant stretch of skin. The caterer jolted, twisting back. Her spine hit the mattress and the woman pinned her collarbone, straddling her pelvis, thighs bearing down on thighs.

"What are you doing?" The caterer's voice broke, nearly laughing. Her hands were caught over her zipper, wedged under the woman's bare cunt.

"I'm helping," the woman whispered. "Illuminating. You're carrying all this confusion here." She massaged beneath the caterer's clavicle. "And here." Up and around the shoulders, into the fascia. The caterer lay tense. She sucked her bottom lip as the woman unbuttoned her vest. One by one. Outside, there was music. The woman's fingers worked slow as she peeled the vest open. She traced the shirt's waxy stains.

"This isn't happening," the caterer giggled. She closed her eyes and shifted her hips. The woman tightened her thighs.

"Exactly. You'd never do this." She fingered gaps between the caterer's buttons. "You'd never load up your tray with your favorite little savories and decide it's your turn to have them all for yourself. But even if you didn't hide in the kitchen, if you claimed a spot in the middle of the dining room, who would bother to stop you?" She tugged the stiff bow tie. "Who could?"

"That's wrong," the caterer panted. "You have to unsnap it." The woman's hand found the tie's metal clip. "Be quick."

"No." The woman set to work on the shirt buttons. "Never quick." From the throat to the sternum. "You take care with unwrapping cubes of butter, stacking them, one by one, in rolls of bread. Your teeth glide through slowly, and you breathe through the ache in your belly. That's the only way to test your limits—how much your body can hold." The caterer's breasts, furrowed in stretch marks, sloped to the sides of her bra. "And it will surprise you, your capacity for hunger, your eagerness to lap the roux drying on abandoned plates. You know you should stop when your blood goes thick." The caterer inhaled. Under her rib cage, her stomach was hollow and soft. "Your wrists and ankles leaden, sugar-stunned. When do you realize you can't stand? Admit it's long after you notice the new weight of your belly, the sphere surging into your lap. You wouldn't recognize it as yours if it weren't for the throbbing. You, expansive, filling space. Every cell vibrating, heating, and it will hurt when you stop, but not yet, not these last seconds before you pulse into air." She opened the last button above the tight waistband. She bit the plush of each hip. "Is that when everyone notices you? Your skin stretched so taut you might just rip open—look how far you've tested the knot."

Her thumb hooked into the caterer's navel. Pressed where the skin puckered and where it pulled flat. The caterer gasped, her tendons seizing as the woman tongued up her rib cage, folded back the cups of her bra. Her nipples were tawny pink, ringed with sparse hairs. The woman circled the left areola with her tongue. She drew it into her mouth, tasting sweat and detergent, and sucked, then sucked harder, dislodging sebum. She licked the nipple and deepened her thumb. The caterer moaned, fingers twitching under the woman's cunt. They groped through her hair.

"No, no," the woman said, voice muffled. She ground her pubic bone against knuckles. "Greedy girl. That's not what you want."

Another moan, louder. The caterer nipped at the woman's wrist. The woman slid her forearm to the mouth. They bit down in unison. The caterer clamped to bone. The woman gnawed, shifting layers, parting muscle and skin.

Outside, the song faded. The woman parted her teeth, then her lips. She lifted her face and straightened her spine. The areola was purple, etched by her incisors. She watched it deflate. The caterer opened her eyes and spit the woman's arm out.

"Wait," she whimpered, "that's it?"

"I came to enjoy the party. And listen—" Through the window, there was cheering, whistling, whooping. "The groom has kissed the bride."

"Shit," the caterer hissed, flying upright. She fumbled with her buttons, grabbed her bow tie. "Shit, shit, shit."

"Thank god—I'm starving."

"The makeup. Bullshit."

The woman bared her teeth. "Do you see something lodged in the front here? Ah." She plucked a thin hair from her canine. "This was yours—make a wish."

And, blowing a kiss, she stepped out into the hallway. She looked toward the bright dining room, toward voices lifted in greeting. Sharper sounds too. Complaints. An argument. She touched the swell on her lips and joined the budding crowd.

*S*he had lied to the caterer, but only by half. At the mansion on the mountain, she'd tended to delicate grooming with her delicate hands. She'd been provided all the right tools, finely made and clean. She'd had a room. A canopy bed and claw-foot bath and rosewood vanity with its oval mirror. Shawls and trinkets imitating clutter. The room didn't bother with clocks or passing light. On her walls, there hung one set of heavy curtains and one grand painting—a white swan in oils, floating on gray. It gazed over the room with a hard, black eye.

The woman heard the chimes, and her bedroom walls were sage. She draped a silk robe over her bare shoulders. Next to the bathtub, she found bottles and jars and small metal instruments arranged on a brass tray. There, too, she found a note card with her instructions. The woman read the neat lines, the fine script. She perched by the taps and ran a hot bath. She sprinkled the basin with salts and oils, anise and heather. The water steamed. She waited.

Another chime, then knocking. "Come in," she called. "The door is unlocked."

A girl entered slowly, tall, bronze, and glowing, hair piled in a riotous bun. Her dress skimmed the floor.

"Wait." The woman spun the taps shut. "Leave your clothing there."

The girl nodded. She breathed through her nostrils, exhaling little. She removed her slippers. She pulled down her dress. Her breasts, like her limbs, were long and slender. Black hair ran from the spout of her belly button, pooling over her cunt. It coated her knees and calves and ankles. She'd painted her toenails teal. She cracked her knuckles against the floor.

When the girl spoke, her voice was soft. "I shaved my armpits."

"I didn't ask," said the woman.

"They were driving me crazy."

"I didn't ask." The woman rolled up her sleeves. She skated her fingers over the bathwater. "It's warm."

The girl stepped one foot into the basin, then the other. The water swayed. She folded her limbs and sank slowly, exhaling. She kept her neck dry.

"No bubbles?" she asked, peering at her floating breasts. Her nipples drifted outward, areolas soft and wide.

"I need to see you."

"Right. It's nice anyway." She hugged her knees. "Thank you."

The woman pulled the tray to her hip. She tapped a squat tin, then twisted its cap in slow half circles. Its toffee salve smelled like eucalyptus and rosemary. "Give me your legs. Both of them."

The girl shifted, hooking her knees over the edge of the tub, careful not to splash. Still steady on the basin's lip, the woman set the girl's wet feet in her lap. She massaged both calves with salve. Beneath thick hair, the girl's skin was soft. A mole poked from her right calf. It was a perfect circle, red and raised. The salve made it glisten. When the woman swiped her hands under the crook of each knee, the girl fidgeted. Water sloshed and spilled.

"Okay," the girl said. "All right."

The woman squeezed the girl's feet, and then her own hips, smearing excess salve on her robe. She lifted a gold razor from the tray. It flipped open with a single snap of her wrist, the blade sharp and square and long as her palm.

She dipped the blade into the bathwater. She lifted it to the girl's knee.

"Keep your eyes open."

The girl nodded, her nostrils flaring. The woman ran the razor down the long left calf. She traced the girl's femur. With each pass, the blade gathered hair and dead skin, a caterpillar of tissue. The woman rinsed residue into the water again and again. She angled the razor up and down each ankle and pivoted over each knee. She cupped the girl's heels, lifting to reach behind her calves.

As hair fell away, marks on the girl's skin emerged. Scarce freckles. A waxy scar on her ankle. Stripes faded down inner thighs. A knotted vein behind the left knee, flinching under the razor. The blade hummed along stray lines of stubble. The girl's chest rose and fell, slower now, nearly silent. A film of hair bobbed around her breasts.

"Stand up," the woman said. She brushed the blade against her lap as the girl uncoiled from the water. The wet hair on her upper thighs was finer, already soft. Leaning forward, teetering, the woman shaved the spare patches away. Then, she worked salve over the girl's belly and drew the razor down, stopping when she reached the girl's mound.

"Okay," the girl said. The muscles below her ribs tightened. Her kneecaps twitched.

The woman looked up at the girl's face. Steam had melted her mascara, smattering black around her sockets. She blinked and held her body still. Nodding, the woman swapped her razor for a small pair of gold scissors.

"Spread your legs," she said.

The girl stared at the scissors. She slid her feet apart, opening a dimpled triangle between her thighs. A smell like mulch drifted from her vulva. Dense hair curled over her mound and down her labia. It grew long.

The woman pinched a tuft from the girl's mound and stretched it taut. The roots strained against their follicles. Crouching, she posed the scissors, suspending them a half centimeter from the girl's skin. She snipped downward, slowly. Each cut was measured and precise. Hair fell away. Clumps scattered in the bathwater or clung to the girl's kneecaps. Strands wrapped around the woman's knuckles, slid behind her fingernails. The scissors made the room's only sound.

At the outer labia, the woman slowed further, floating her blades along the curve of each tender lobe. She tilted from the basin's ledge. She twisted her shoulders. Finally, she slid to her knees, setting her eyeline between the girl's thighs. She reached underneath to part the girl's hair. She eased lobe from lobe. Their bodies created shadows. It was difficult to tell hair from flesh. Starting left, the woman aligned fingers against labium, scissors against fingers. She pinched and pulled. She cut. The blades grazed her knuckles. She snipped. Then again, with meticulous attention to the bottommost curve, the inner edges, the slope climbing toward the perineum. Then the right lobe. The girl did not flinch or tremble or breathe, and the woman did not cut her.

13

When the scissors could trim no closer, the woman set them aside and turned the faucet to a trickle. "Rinse," she said. "Let's see what's left."

The girl gathered water in her cupped palms. She splashed her hips and thighs until they were clean. The woman watched and rocked her neck. She shut off the tap. Flecks of hair frothed back to the surface. They surrounded the girl's calves in rings.

"Very still," the woman said. She coated the pads of her fingers with salve. She anointed the girl's remaining hair, massaging slowly, down and back and up again, each fingertip kneading a tight spiral. The salve warmed and thinned, soaking every bristle. The woman daubed lingering balm on the backs of her hands. She gelled the edges of her scalp.

The second razor was smaller than the first, but no less square. Its blade was light and thin. The woman rested its edge above the girl's mound. She pressed a soft line. She scraped down, following the hair's grain, shaving close, leaving stubble. She flipped the blade and stroked upward, cutting down to the follicle. Roots flicked against gold. The girl's mound lay smooth and brown.

The woman paused. She wiped the razor with her sleeve. "Sit on the edge of the tub," she said.

"Yes." The girl's voice was small. She bent back into an unsteady seat and exhaled through her teeth. Her shoulders curled forward, her breasts drooping down her ribs.

"Lean back," the woman said. "Touch your shoulders to the wall."

The girl obeyed. She clutched the porcelain by her hips.

"Stretch your legs to me. Set your feet here, on the edge."

The girl suspended herself across the tub. One foot, then the other, her legs drifting slow. The second foot slipped, screeching. The girl bit her lip.

"Wider."

The girl anchored her heels. She spread her thighs, and her cunt's glossy ridges unfurled.

"Set a finger there, in the center."

"I might slip."

"You won't."

The girl's left hand tightened, knuckles blanching. Her right floated up, her arm draping over her belly as she lay her palm on her mound. She curled her index finger down.

"Inside," the woman said.

"Okay," the girl breathed. "Okay." She did not watch her cunt swell over her finger. She did not watch her knuckles disappear.

Kneeling still, the woman brought her face between the girl's knees. She angled her arm. When the blade's dull back brushed against inner thigh, the girl gasped but did not slip. She held steady as the sharp edge crept over her labia, nicking against the stubble's grain, scraping outward in, toward her finger and the fragile tissue it covered. Her cunt flushed hot.

Then, the woman was finished. She inspected her work. The shave was close and clean, and there was no blood. Just as requested. She stood tall over the tub. She pressed her shoulders back.

"Remove your hand."

The girl was breathing evenly. Deep, musical breaths. Her finger pulled viscous threads, white film.

"Stand up. Out of the tub. It's finished."

"May I have a towel?" The girl asked, unsteady on her feet.

"You have your clothes. Get dressed and go."

The woman propped herself up in bed, turning her profile to the painted swan and its eye. She pressed her robe's stains against her sheets. She flexed her hands, examining hatched lines, wrinkled joints. She didn't look up as the girl left, or as the cleaning women entered, hauling their mops and brushes, eager to reset the room. Salve packed her fingernails. She bit the mess away.

*T*he woman watched wedding guests fill the house. Spilling from the dining room down through the sunken living room, they juggled wine and cocktail napkins and gossip, careful to keep elbows from knocking elbows, hips from brushing hips. They wore pastels and gingham, sunscreen and contour, friends and family indistinguishable in this plucked, pale crowd. None questioned her presence there. A few women eyed her bare feet. Another slipped off her heels.

She listened to the aunts and uncles beside her, gossiping over mimosas and cabernet and plastic cups, slippery in moist fingers, *the taste already leaching in.* They agreed it made no sense, the shortage of coffee. *If they're going to insist on such an early wedding,* they exclaimed. *Or—I'll say it—late.* Laughter rolling. *Can't you let that go for one single day? Times have changed. Thank god Mom's not here to see it. Baby bump in a white dress.* Heads nodding and shaking. *Oh, if you're so bothered, don't look at her from the side.*

Other guests had picked up the disposable cameras. The woman watched a stooped grandfather photograph the slideshow. A mother arranged her children on a love seat, hand in hand for one photo, boy-lips to girl-cheek for two more. The boy wore a tiny suit; the girl, a cupcake dress. They did as they were told.

The woman moved to the dining room's windowed wall. Her fingerprints kissed the hot glass. Outside, the backyard was square and fenced and treeless, and the caterer rushed to help her teammates roll tables onto the manicured lawn. Across the grass, the bridal party posed chest to back. Six bridesmaids, all cinched waists and lilac satin, angled their chins toward a professional photographer's professional lens. In the center stood Michaela, full and rosy, draped in a bell of white tulle. Rhinestones dusted her empire bodice. They matched the sterling leaves pinning her hair. The women positioned their bouquets against their stomachs. Their cheekbones were polished. When they smiled, they gleamed.

Next came family. The bride's mother, blonde, thick, and giddy, her stilettos puncturing the grass. The bride's father, his wide hands pressed over his heart. The bride's stepmother behind him in a muted blue dress, waving at Charlotte to hurry—Charlotte, drowning in tea party chiffon, lavender faded and sagging off her tensed shoulders, bones jutting through ashen skin. Her smile was pinched. Her cheeks had been polished too.

The woman had not expected Charlotte. In the hours before they met, she had been walking further down the mountain. Away from the mansion and other messes that opened and entered her skin. The sky had been black, tinted navy. She walked slow and alone through the night.

She passed through hot, quiet streets, past houses on private acres, fences run through with poison ivy and blackberry, chain link warping to forest. A chill seeped through the redwoods. Damp bark and damp ferns. Deer and asphalt. Oil slicks and oil glands and nerves. She reached the throat of a two-lane highway and a dark gas station. Four pumps and a convenience store, walls painted like logs. Behind fluorescent beer signs and lotto jackpots, the windows were black. There was still some time before dawn.

The woman squatted on a pump's concrete base, her knees spread toward the empty highway, her skirt crumpled to the crease of her hips. A mosquito flitted over her kneecap, down her inner thigh. She watched it pierce her. She watched it fly away. The bite crackled under a thread of cool air, and she arched her cunt to the breeze. She felt the freshly torn blisters on her heels. Grime caked her right hand, binding in her nicked fingertips. Blood and sweat stiffened on her chest. She spat into her palm and rubbed her breastbone. Worked an even stain over her skin.

There was a car on the highway, descending, slowing. The woman petted her neck and watched yellow headlights bump over the curb. She tasted the stale whiskey behind her teeth, felt the diamond teardrops tugging her ears. She did not turn as the car pulled in behind her, alongside the store. She heard a door, then a curse. A high, round voice. Angry and young.

The voice gasped. "Who's there?"

The woman set her palms on the ground.

"I see you moving. I see you. I have mace."

The woman sighed and stood, turning. Her skirt fell past her knees.

"Oh." The girl grumbled something unintelligible. "Is their restroom open?"

"No. But I won't look if you use a tree."

Such a small girl, Charlotte, thin beneath her college sweatshirt, hands hidden in stained sleeves. Above her car's lights, her face was pallid and hollow. Pimples roughed her cheeks. She picked pus from her chin.

"That's okay. No thank you. Have a good night—morning—who knows—"

"I was promised mace," the woman said.

"I don't have any," she blurted. "I thought you were a guy."

"I need a ride."

Charlotte chewed on her thumbnail. Shadows stretched under her eyes. "I'm not sure."

"I don't much like asking for help, but I'm alone out here, and I'm hurt." The woman stepped closer, holding out her bloodied hand.

"Jesus Christ." Charlotte turned away. "You could...Do you want my phone? To call someone?"

"I want you to drive me down the mountain."

"I don't think I can."

"You don't think you *should*." The woman sweetened her voice. "It's not that I don't understand—you've been drilled about danger and rightly so. You're tired and it's risky, offering help to a stranger, and anyway I can keep resting right here until they open or the next driver pulls in. Sunday morning—maybe I'll luck out with a lonely trucker. You head on your way. There's no reason to worry about me."

Charlotte groaned. She slapped the roof of her car. Mosquitos scattered. "Fine. Fine. Get in."

The woman settled into the passenger seat. She smelled something curdled wafting from the cushions and then, as they drove, through the dash. A dingy chiffon dress hung over a back window, still thrift-store tagged. Gum wrappers, air plug-ins, and a purple card rustled under her feet. She picked up the invitation and read its embossed script. *Jordan & Michaela seal their sacred bond. Joined in marriage by the Bride's Proud Father, Greg.* The girl offered up her own name then too, shoving a piece of gum into her mouth and smacking. Aspartame and peppermint and benzoyl peroxide. The woman cracked her window. She lifted her face.

"I didn't expect company." Charlotte hunched over the steering wheel. "Sorry. This is one hundred percent a mistake."

They turned under the pull-off's lone streetlamp. Light washed down the dash and over Charlotte's shredded cuticles, her nail beds raw and red. Her ponytail was pulled tight, brown hair thin over white scalp. She wound the car through a tunnel of redwoods. Their headlights bounced. The road's borders flashed white and yellow. Caution signs and dented guardrails. The sudden curve above a ravine.

Charlotte exhaled. "Sorry. Someone stole my stereo."

"Stop apologizing," the woman said. "There are other ways to pass the time."

"I guess so."

The woman watched Charlotte shift and clench her thighs.

"We still have a long drive ahead of us. Pull over. I'll watch the car."

"I can hold it."

"Suit yourself."

Something crashed in the forest. Charlotte's jaw popped. She swallowed her gum.

The woman tapped the invitation. "Charlotte, Charlotte. So young to have friends getting married."

Charlotte snorted. "Michaela's my stepsister. Jordan is," she bit at her middle finger, "who she settled for. And anyway, they finished college. They're old." She tore a hangnail and cringed.

"You don't seem so excited."

"I tried to just send a playlist, but my mom said—wait. I shouldn't tell you things."

"You might like how I listen."

"I won't."

"Aren't you boring."

"I'm driving you to the hospital. Should I stop? Or if you want to talk, how about explaining what you did to your hand?"

"That's fair, I suppose. Something happened. Some minor calamity led me to your car. Which do you like best? First, I lied. I didn't cut my hand. A man invited me over for sex. While he ate me out, I got my period. He spit and promised he wasn't upset. After he came, he saw his bloodied sheet and asked me if I could please clean it. He pointed me toward gloves, a brush, bleach. I slicked my blood off his cock and left.

"Second option. I lied. A man invited me over for sex. In reality, he wanted my menstrual underwear. He'd tracked my cycle, he said. I had no underwear to offer. I pulled out my cup and held it to his mouth instead. The cup was full. As he sipped, some blood dribbled. He asked if I felt a fresh clot coming. I folded the cup back inside me and left.

"You'll like this one. A man invited me over for sex. He handed me a knife, and I opened my palm. The blade was sharp. It sliced clean. And the gash was just long enough for his cock to rest end to end. It settled along the cut. My blood warmed. He came until his lips lost their color. And I left."

Charlotte's mouth twisted, her pelvis sucked tight to her seat.

The woman continued, "Which do you think?"

"I was trying to help you."

"Then help me. Where have I been? Which way do you lean?"

"If you're planning to murder me, get it over with."

"And ruin your sister's big day?"

"Yeah right. She's already pregnant." She bit her lip. "Shit." And started a new piece of gum.

The redwood canopy broke open. The navy sky had a green luster. A pair of eyes sparked white in the headlights, disappeared in the brush. Charlotte sat close and closed, her mouth flat, eyes dark walls.

The woman tutted. "Snitching on your sister."

"Stepsister."

"When you fuck, does she tattle on you?"

Charlotte gave no answer.

"Perhaps she won't report what's imaginary. When you touch yourself, is that how you curl?"

"Fuck off."

The woman could smell something new. Something sharp and heady—spoiling citrus. She rolled the car window up.

"Ah, you're not so blank, Charlotte. Don't pretend."

They sped onward. The edges of the windshield collected steam.

"For example," she continued, "you know Michaela is fucking Jordan. She brought him home for Christmas, shared a bed in the room next to yours. In the middle of the night, your bed trembled. Still, they were silent. So quiet that you held your breath. And what then? Do you press your ear to the wall? What do you play before you dream?"

"I'm not talking to you."

"No. You're stubborn. You don't want to know why you picked me up. You don't want to go to this wedding. You don't

23

want to pee. And you're good at this—you've practiced shutting down. So, let's look away, out a bit further. I'll talk, and when I'm finished, you'll tell me what's true."

"I'm not playing," Charlotte said.

The woman went on, her voice easy. "Like you, this girl had a stepsister. But she was younger—only twelve and innocent for her age. Innocent even for her small private school. She hadn't yet developed your little sheen of bitterness. She was too naïve to know she didn't know. Can you remember such a time? Imagine. Don't romanticize. Because, even innocent, our girl was beginning to sense some sort of something—a shift she couldn't put into words.

"There was also the influence of her stepsister. Fifteen, attending a public school with no uniforms. Wearing her t-shirts tight and her eyeliner smudged. She had so few rules and still, when the parents forbade her from piercing her navel, she'd done it just the same. Now, she often fiddled with the steel bar, twisting the cubic zirconia, her fingers sliding up and under those shirts. The student could not watch this. She pictured the hoop sliding too far inside, scraping against all that human jelly. It made her throat dry."

Charlotte rolled the car windows down. Wind rushed in. The woman grew loud.

"One night, the stepsister was restless. She flopped on the sofa in the finished basement, interrupting the student's flash cards, kicking the cushions, yelling that she was bored. She wore soft blue shorts and a thin blue t-shirt, tight against the cups of her bra. *Homework time is over*, she announced. They should be bonding. They should play M.A.S.H.

"When her first round did not reunite her with her ex-boyfriend, the stepsister flung herself backward, exposing the crystal in her belly. The student looked away and made her list of future husbands. Handsome actors. The cute boy in her class. Her stepsister repeated this last one, smirking.

'You finally have a crush.'

'Me and every girl in my grade.'

'Oh, competition,' the stepsister cooed. 'Fun.' She tapped the pen around the M.A.S.H. page until the student found herself fated to fifteen kids, a shack, and the boy from her class. She suspected her stepsister had forced that final result. It wasn't worth pointing out. They both laughed as she folded their game between the cushions of the couch.

Her stepsister sat up straighter, crossing her thighs. 'So, you still don't have a boyfriend.'

The student felt the appraisal, the assessment of the gold cross on her neck and the center part of her hair. She wanted to explain. *At my school, things are different. Only the kids who get detention mess around.* But the truth was she knew about classmates disappearing at recess. She was aware of pairs running after the bell, lips swollen and collars bent. Not to mention that seventh-grade girls shaved their legs. They rolled their skirts and wore spandex shorts over their underwear. Boys trailed them up the stairs.

The student rolled her eyes. 'You're just mad that guy dumped you.'

'That's hilarious. *I* dumped *him*. I had to—he sucked at sex.'

'You had sex?'

'I guess that means you haven't. I bet you haven't even kissed.'

'I'm not a teenager.'

'I had two boyfriends at your age.'

'I'm saving myself until marriage,' the student said. She burned to the tips of her ears.

Her stepsister rocked as she laughed. 'Oh my god, you actually say that. I mean, I've heard girls say they said it, but wow—you used those exact words. And guess what—it's hilarious—today, every one of those girls is a slut.' She clutched her chest, wheezing, sliding down to the beige carpet. 'Actually, one of them taught me the best game. We're going to play.'

The student gazed down at her stepsister's hair, the strands matted with unrinsed conditioner, the smell like coconuts and sunscreen and shoulders on the beach. Other girls in her grade said the marriage pledge and meant it. She knew they did. They'd all heard it so early and often that the words felt true in their mouths. She watched her stepsister pick up their ballpoint pen and tensed, picturing the girls in her class talking under the basketball hoops, pigeon-toed in tight circles, pleated hems brushing midthigh. She pictured the man who, just last week, had whistled at her from his car. She had been standing at a crosswalk. No one had ever hit on her before.

'It's called The Pen Test. All you have to do is pull down your panties and stick the pen up there. If the pen stops, you're a virgin. If it goes'—the stepsister's voice lilted, singsong—'you're a lying little slut. Because that means some guy popped your cherry.' She wagged the pen. '*Broke* your *hymen*. Are you really this dumb?'

'You want to put the pen in me?'

'Oh my god,' the stepsister groaned. 'No. You're going to put it in you. Pretend it's a weird, long tampon. Wait, have you never used a tampon? Wow. Okay.' She leaned forward, mouth open. 'You haven't touched yourself down there, just a little? Just once?'

The student's stomach constricted, her throat too dry to answer. There was the quick pressure through toilet paper. A tug on new curls. Did those count? She wanted to pinch her stepsister's midriff until it bruised.

'Maybe I shouldn't do this.'

The stepsister rolled her eyes. 'Jesus won't care about a pen. Get down here.'

Sighing, the student slumped to the floor. 'Are you going to look at me?'

'That's literally part of the game.' The stepsister stripped off her pajama shorts. 'Don't be weird—it's a sleepover. We're both girls.' She tossed her thong between them. Blue satin splotched white. She spread her legs, and the student saw stubble, smelled salt. She remembered a xeroxed diagram passed around the special health class, that week they'd separated girls and boys. Monochrome ovals. Flat lines. *Hymen* neatly labeled. *Fallopian. Vulva.* But they'd gotten the textures all wrong.

'Like this.' The stepsister spread herself with two fingers. Her other hand flipped the pen, held it by its ballpoint tip. She pressed the flat base between her labia, and with an inhale, she pushed. Plastic slid, one inch, two. In and up. Further. It slid deep.

'I fail.' She giggled and pulled the pen free. 'But I mean, I think I win.' Something slick and clear coated the smooth plastic. She wiped it with the hem of her shirt. There were two rough red lines on her hip. A flat brown mole where hip met thigh. The student took the pen. It was warm and made unfamiliar. Much like the rest of this basement, much like her underwear's worn pastel cotton, the thick elastic waistband. She wriggled her legs free, and her stepsister giggled again. The student grew determined. She tilted her pelvis. She imagined the thing inside her, this internal freshness seal. How did she pee? She knew the diagram had taught this and did not want to remember, did not want to be distracted in her search for her own silt smell. But nothing. Her body was a blank, and now this test would confirm it. Nothing smudged or split or missing. Her stomach sank and tightened. She took hold of the pen the wrong way, pointed down. She aimed. She thought she might push the tip hard.

'Hey. Don't get ink in your cooch.'

'Oh. Right.' The student cleared her throat and turned the pen over. She aimed the blunt end and pushed and gasped. She had not predicted this pliant tissue, the shock of the first shallow tap. She did not look as she rooted for center but wondered at the buzzing along her gumline, the pins pricking her scalp. The pen hit a curved ridge. She shuddered. A rod of static rippled behind her belly button. What was the motion? In. And up.

'Okay,' her stepsister said, 'you're a virgin. Stop masturbating.'

The student froze. 'I'm not,' she mumbled. She blinked back vertigo, shifted her hand. The pen slid deep.

They gasped then in unison. There was not pain but instead the sensation of her tongue on the roof of her mouth. No pain even as she yanked the pen, none despite the scraping plastic seam and her own dripping film, bloodless, clear. The carpet itched the backs of her thighs. She saw the imprint of its tufts. She saw her legs open on the beige carpet and the curls between her legs and she didn't know what happened, she said. She had barely moved her hand. Her stepsister had retrieved her shorts and was standing, kicking into each leg. *I know there's no way you've had sex,* she said. *There's no way.* The student brushed a fiber from her ankle and felt again her tingling scalp. So there was a circuitry. She wondered if her smell would follow, and when, and she reached for her shorts, catching nothing her stepsister said. *I asked who's been messing around with you! Or else, oh my god, did you have to push so fucking hard?* Had she pushed hard? That wasn't supposed to be how it worked.

The student wanted this to be over. She started to cry, and then she was on the couch, her head in her stepsister's lap. Her stepsister shushed her, stroking her forehead, her part. It was the closest they had ever been. The student felt thigh bones pressing her skull and the folded edge of M.A.S.H. grazing her lumbar and the thin blue t-shirt and the piercing poking her cheek. She heard her stepsister's cloudy voice.

'It's okay. It's all okay. I mean, we don't even know if anything happened tonight. Or before tonight—not that I'm saying there's something you did. Just don't say anything to my mom. *Nothing* to your mom. Or your dad. I don't mean lie— just—it's a sleepover secret, okay? Between sisters.' She hooked their pinkies to seal the promise. 'Nothing really happened anyway. There's no way it counts.'

The student sniffled and nodded. Her stepsister's nails raked her scalp.

'One of my friends swears hers popped on the jungle gym. Maybe that's what happened to you.'

Her voice thickened in her throat. She grabbed the TV remote, clicking aimlessly. Commercials flickered over their faces, green and gray and blue. The speakers were loud, but the student could hear her stepsister's breath slowing. She nestled into the thin blue shirt. Its hem rose. There was thudding in her ears and the static pressure spreading through her core. The light skipped blue to green, green to gold, and as the zirconia flashed, she smelled summer. She lifted her tongue to the salt."

Outside the car, the sky was streaked with fuchsia, bordered by the jagged silhouette of the trees. While the woman spoke, the wind had built and died, built and died, warming. Still, Charlotte shivered. She spit her gum out the window. Rolled the windows up and sucked the spittle from her chin.

"I don't want to kiss my stepsister."

The woman stared, drawing closer. "Is that all you heard?"

"Oops. Guess I didn't listen."

"Is that what you tell Michaela?"

"Get out of my car."

"Pull over. Oh, but you won't, will you." The woman swept her hand toward the forest pressing around them. "If you stop the car here, in this nowhere, what will I do?"

Charlotte hunched further, her mouth again a firm line, her face straight toward the road. The air smoldered. The woman took in that sharp smell.

"Poor thing, always pouting. I hope you savor it. Because there's something circling, Charlotte, something that makes your throat itch."

Charlotte was silent, vibrating. The woman drew toward her.

"Tell me what you want."

"To drive off this cliff."

"I can't stop you."

"No."

But the car remained steady on the road. They rounded a broad curve, and sunrise stretched over the approaching valley. Charlotte's chin and her chest and her thighs were silent, taut, pulsing. The woman smiled, nestling back into her headrest, reaching into her hair. She dropped the diamond earrings into a cupholder, propping her bare feet on the dash. They were arched and tarred, blisters raw, nails shredded. She crossed her ankles. Her big toe sketched a heart. She watched Charlotte's face hold sallow in the sunlight, eyes set firmly away from her feet.

"Charlotte, Charlotte," the woman said. "You're so nearly no fun."

The mountain sloped and flattened, and the highway broke open, two lanes to four, four to eight. Other cars droned beside them, passengers blurred behind glass. The woman watched a wrinkled man nod off and jerk awake. When his eyes closed, he licked his teeth.

Charlotte had driven on and on, her speed steady, her mouth packed with gum. She signaled when she changed lanes. She signaled when she took her exit and pulled up alongside a diner. And again, that blinking signal as the woman stood in the overgrown parking lot, watching her drive away. It was true morning then, clear blue daylight. The woman snapped sour grass from the edge of the sidewalk. She chewed, sucking tart from the stem. She remembered the address in its cursive. Barefoot, her pace measured, she'd followed Charlotte's first turn.

And now, the woman stood at the dining room's wide windows, watching Charlotte pose with the bride. Charlotte's bodice gaped around her chest. She placed her hand on her hip, her bicep no larger than her wrist. She smiled through thin lips and looked anywhere but the camera. When her gaze drifted toward the window, she scowled but stood frozen. The photographer shooed her away. Clutching her bodice, she broke across the lawn. The woman watched her nudge through the guests. Her hair hung in rigid waves, her smell chemical. Powder caked her cheeks.

"Leave," Charlotte spat. "Now."

"You were so kind to extend the invitation. I'm having a marvelous time."

"You don't get to do this." Charlotte wore a press-on French manicure, gummy pink tipped with white. She pushed her hair behind her ears.

"I see you found the diamonds—how they suit you. You should keep the shoes I left too. Do they fit? I borrowed your pearls."

"You weren't supposed to be here."

"At least I think they're yours. It's your room they're turning into an office? The one with that hard, chilly bed?"

"I'm going to call the police."

The woman tsked. "Well, that would put an end to the party. You'll have a lot to explain to your family. Do you know you look just like your mother? Go on, tell her how you met me. I wonder which words you'll use."

Charlotte closed her eyes. There was a ladder of bones in her chest. It lifted as she sighed.

"Why are you doing this?"

"Oh, dear one." She cupped Charlotte's cheek. "Don't you know your skin's warm?"

The girl recoiled.

"People are staring."

"Are they?" She turned, searching over her shoulder.

"Stop looking at people. Don't touch them or talk to them, not anyone, and especially don't say one single word to my mother. You have ten minutes before I tell everyone who you are."

Metal tinged against glass. The bride's father stood at the half wall, wine and fork raised high. Greg had a pasty complexion and heavy jaw. Broad shoulders and trim waist and a tailored gray suit. Silver cuff links. Tight slacks. The woman found the outline of his cock.

"Family and friends, please join me in welcoming Mr. and Mrs. Jordan Thompson!" He swung the knife toward the front of the house. The bride's skirts swirled into the living room. Someone roared, *Give her a kiss!* The guests whistled and clapped as the groom dipped her low and complied.

Now, Greg announced, it was time to eat, *to celebrate and mingle and remember the unifying power of love.* The silver serving troughs opened to wet eggs, wet sausage, wet potato in pale cubes. Guests surged forward with white paper china and silver plastic forks. Others embraced the couple, crowding to shake hands and kiss cheeks. Greg stood behind Michaela, holding her bare biceps. He kissed the golden crown of her head. He said something to Jordan, something short and smirking. The men slapped each other's shoulders. The space between their bodies made a box. And then the woman saw Greg see her. She saw his grin falter and shine.

Charlotte weaved through the dining room to her mother, tall and narrow in her blue sheath, gray streaked through cropped brown hair. Charlotte grabbed her forearm. She spoke quickly, her hands flapping toward the woman at the window. Her mother shook her head. She tugged at Charlotte's loose bodice, pinching the fabric around the zipper, forcing the spine straight. She pulled the girl down the hall. The woman smelled yolks and pig fat and something like urine or fresh-cut grass. She saw the caterer outside, sweating, placing the last bouquet on the last table. She waved.

*I*n the mansion on the mountain, the woman had paced and dozed. Time likely passed. The chimes sounded, and the woman opened her eyes to persimmon walls. She sighed and stretched and rubbed her toes. She draped her silk robe over her shoulders. She studied the tools on her tray: black ribbon, capped needles, small sterling balls, and small sterling hoops open wide. A decanter blown from dark green glass. The note card, its elegant letters. A tube of cherry red lipstick. The woman stood in front of the swan and painted her mouth. A thick, glossy coat. The chimes sounded. A girl arrived.

Another girl, this one older, shorter, her skin pale cream. She had straight shoulders and straight hips and her own silk robe cinching a slim waist.

"Nice outfit," the girl said. She shimmied her sleeves.

"Undress," the woman said. She dragged a wooden chair from the corner. Silk cushions, embroidered orchids. She traced gold threads up their stems.

"Am I early?" the girl asked. "The door was unlocked. I'm happy to wait. Take your time."

"Undress," the woman said. "The door is always unlocked."

The girl nodded. "It's cold. I'd like a drink."

The woman pulled a stool out from under her vanity. She set it in front of her chair, next to her tray. She lifted the dark decanter.

"Okay," she said. "Open your mouth."

The girl did. The woman poured. And drank too, a deep swill. Something like honey dripped down their chins.

"Woof," the girl said. "What was that? Wow."

The woman shrugged. "Undress."

"Of course I don't ask until after. I guess I'd be easy to poison. If my mother was right about one thing—"

"Stop talking." The woman shed her robe. Naked, she stepped toward the girl. She pinched her silk collar. The girl's breath was hot and floral. She undressed. Tattoos swirled down her fair skin. Peonies down her right shoulder. Fangs at her elbow. A lunar moth beneath high, firm breasts. Her stomach was bare. Her hips too. She had smooth thighs and a short cock. She pointed to the tattoo above her knee.

"This one's my favorite," she said. A Victorian hand, holding a dagger.

"Lovely," the woman said. "Sit."

"It's really cold in here."

"Sit. Straddle the back of the chair. Yes, like that. You will sit there, silent, and hold yourself upright."

"I've handled needles before."

"You'll have no breaks. If you ask, I'll work slower."

"Perfect," the girl said. She fell quiet.

"Good girl," the woman said, arranging herself on her stool. She looked over the girl's back, white excepting the edges of pink petals. "You wouldn't want me to puncture a muscle."

She placed her lips on the girl's chilled skin. A kiss to the right of the spine, high under the shoulder blade. Her lips left a red stamp. She kissed again, lower, and again, working closer to the spine and away. Ten horizontal kisses on the right and ten on the left, exactly mirrored, sketching an hourglass. The girl shivered.

"Are you going to warn me as you go?" she asked.

"No."

The woman picked up a needle and tossed the plastic cap aside. The needle itself was steel, hollow and thick. The woman rested it below the girl's nape, between vertebrae, rolling its weight. Goosebumps climbed her neck.

"Not losing your nerve?" the woman said.

The girl shook her head.

"Hold still."

The woman took her time. She opened the decanter and rinsed the needle, sloshing alcohol over the floor. Steel glinted in the rusty light. With one hand, she gripped a pad of flesh on the girl's low back, collapsing the print of her lips. Pinching and lifting. Unsticking from muscle and bone. She aimed the needle at the collapsed red lip print, lay its point in cupid's bow. The girl exhaled. And the woman pierced down, breaking the skin, easing her grip as the needle worked under and along and back up. The point emerged from the center of her stamped cherry mouth. There was no blood. She paused, suspending metal in tissue. She hooked an open sterling hoop into the needle. An exact match. She steadied her hands. And, in one movement, she pulled the needle and pushed the hoop, forced the hoop down and under and up, forced it to sit in the pair of fresh holes. She opened her fingers. The hoop floated in the girl's back. A halo encircled the wounds—pink, then red. The woman reached for a second needle. Nineteen red mouths climbing up the smooth back. Nineteen silver hoops on the tray.

The girl was quiet. She held herself upright.

The woman continued her work. She did not rush. She did not skip out of order. She pierced up the right side, following her marks toward the spine and away. Sometimes, the hoop followed the needle in but not out, and the woman had to rock it under the skin, searching for the second hole. The fifth piercing bled, and the sixth. Blood ran down the girl's back, soaking orchids. The woman did not slow. Her tenth mark rested over the girl's shoulder, where scarce fat did little to guard muscle and bone. She pinched what she could. When she stabbed, the girl winced. She curled her shoulders and clipped a moan. Her jerking pulled her piercings. The bleeding started again. But the needle had made it straight through.

"You're lucky," the woman said. "I have excellent aim."

The girl took a breath. She pulled her shoulders back into place. The woman installed the hoop. Its submerged center pushed up, visible through the girl's soft skin. The girl's right side blotched red. The woman reached for the low fleshy place on the left. The second row, from the bottom up. Each needle broke the skin. Each hoop held it broken. She watched the girl adjust her arms, clutching the back of her chair. The girl's skin began to twitch. The woman pinched harder, forcing patches of skin smooth and still. The fifteenth piercing bled more than the others. The sixteenth bled more than that. Blood strayed down the woman's fingers. She watched a ripple pass down the girl's back. She heard her choked moan.

When she pinched the left shoulder, the girl jerked away. The woman let go. She waited.

"I'm sorry," the girl said. "I won't do it again."

The woman said nothing.

"I'm so sorry. Please go on."

The woman did not.

"Please." Her voice arched. "*Please.*"

The woman scratched down the girl's back with her fingernails. She pinched very close to her spine. Pinched and held. And let go and reached for the left shoulder and clamped the spare flesh. She rested the needle on the cupid's bow. She applied pressure. The skin broke. She pushed slow, barely pushing, watching the thick cylinder glide down, burrowing, swallowing a plug of tissue. She let the needle sit suspended for ten of the girl's long gasps. The hoop, too, entered slowly. It crawled. It slid into place.

The girl looked at the ceiling. Her eyes were open and empty. The woman closed each sterling hoop with a small sterling ball. She leaned back and looked. The silver rows outlined an hourglass, the holes even and inflamed. The woman rinsed them in liquor. The girl writhed. She hissed.

"Your back might feel tender," the woman said. "For a while."

She lifted the black ribbon. It was satin, wide as her pinkie, sleek and long. She threaded it through the highest pair of piercings and pulled it straight across the girl's shoulders, then downward, crisscrossing the spine to the next set of hoops. Lacing the piercings row by row, lacing a corset across the girl's back. At the bottom, the woman tied a bow. The ribbon pulled at the hoops. The hoops pulled at the skin.

"Is it done?" the girl asked, her voice thin. "Can I look?"

"Yes," the woman said.

The girl stood and turned her back to the vanity's mirror. Her face was smooth, her limbs and cock languid, soft, and pink. She craned her neck to her reflection.

"It's wonderful," she said.

The woman picked the girl's robe off the floor. "You'll leave naked."

The girl draped the robe over her arm. "I won't get in trouble?"

"Where do you think you are?" the woman said. "Don't sleep on your back."

The girl laughed, head lolling. She floated out of the room.

The woman stood, still naked, gazing at the tray and the stool and the chair. There were stains in the orchids and the hardwood. There was the taste of alcohol and honey. Then the cleaning women rustling through the door, all garbage bags and bleach, tutting over the upholstery. They scrubbed the floor and her hands. When they left, her knuckles burned, and her throat, and her eyes. The room's set of curtains hung behind her, drawn tight. She parted the heavy panels and stared into plaster. A wall.

*T*here would be the meal, the toasts, the cake, the dancing. That was the order of things. The sun bore down on the backyard. White tablecloths rebounded its glare. The guests shielded their eyes and rearranged their seating. They inhaled tar from the neighbor's new roof. Stripped off their suit jackets and shoulder wraps. Pressed beer bottles against their temples and coaxed condensation down their throats. Bare thighs stuck to wooden chairs.

The woman sat alone near the back fence, between a planter of barbed succulents and a splintering doghouse strung with prayer flags. She sank her thumbnails into an orange. A gift from the caterer, that refrigerated van.

She watched the bridesmaids at the long head table, eating and passing champagne bottles and filling a disposable camera with photos, each waiting to pose with the bride, cheek to cheek. The other half of the table sat vacant, absent its groomsmen and groom. At the family table, Charlotte's seat was empty too. The bride's mother dabbed wine from her lipstick. The bride's father shuffled note cards. The bride's stepmother smoothed his lapel.

The woman spread her knees and inhaled and smelled herself and orange segments cleaving, the juice pricking her scabs. She dug her toes into the cool soil beneath the grass. A young pair asked if they could join her, sitting as far away as the table would allow. They huddled together, muttering. *Next time they go to the garage, I'm joining. I don't care if it's rude. Jordan owes me so much weed.* They took turns glancing her way. In her mouth, polyps burst sweet. She chewed their gristle and seeds. When the fruit was finished, she bit into the peel's soft white underside and, strip by strip, ate the rind.

The young pair gaped. One recovered. "I'm jealous—I only saw juice and mimosas."

The woman swallowed. "You're Jordan's friends?"

"Since high school." The second one's nose was sunburned pink.

"Right after I was his babysitter. How nice. But don't let me co-opt the conversation, unless you're willing to swap memories of our groom? I'm so curious about what he was like in high school. I hope he didn't still have that problem with masturbating, not after I tried to teach him about setting aside private time. No more sneaking in the car or at the library. He even tried it at the dinner table. And trust me, he wasn't fooling around to be funny. He was one insatiable boy." She sighed. "I always wondered if that would change once someone else started touching him. Was it either of you?"

The high school friends darted their eyes at one another, fidgeting. One tittered into a fist.

"Who had the bigger crush on him?" the woman said. "No—I can guess—"

The backyard's speakers thrummed to life. The bride's father tapped a cordless microphone, and the wedding guests turned their heads. A few raised plastic champagne flutes, and the groomsmen, suddenly in their places, whooped and ate. Jordan spoke into Michaela's hair. She giggled and met his kiss. From the family table, Charlotte stared at the woman, arms folded. The woman brought her hands to the crooks of her elbows. She softly pinched the inner folds. Tissue stretched and slid.

"Hello again, friends and family, treasured guests. I hope you'll bear with my voice a bit longer, because believe it or not, I have the honor of officiating and giving the first toast," Greg boomed, his face sun-ruddy, bloated by his smile. "It's an incredible day, and once again I want to thank you for gathering to share in our family's happiness. We know you were invited on short notice, but we managed the summer wedding, and we're honored you're here to support Michaela and Jordan as they begin their new life. They make a beautiful couple, don't they?"

The guests applauded. Their heads bobbed as they cheered. Two roofers appeared atop the neighbor's house, eating sandwiches. They sat on the slanted sheathing and watched.

The bride's father laughed. "Settle down now—they're both taken," he said. He patted one hand over his heart. "I know it must hurt to be a single guy watching this young man bat so far out of his league. I'm teasing, I'm teasing. I'm proud to call Jordan my son-in-law, especially today. He might not be paying rent, but at least he really can comb his hair!"

He paused for the groomsmen's raucous laughter. At the head table, Jordan wrapped his arm around Michaela's shoulders and pulled her close. They grinned together, shaking their heads.

"I know, I know, I promised to take it easy on the jokes. That's right—my own daughter gave me some rules. I'm not going to list them for this angry mob, no way." He chuckled, his teeth large and bleached. "In truth, I'm so happy to welcome Jordan into my family and gather all of you beautiful, sweaty people in my backyard. It's sweltering, isn't it? And there's Susan, mouthing *I told you so*. I still know her so well! Everyone, give it up for Susie, the beautiful bride's beautiful mother, who ran herself ragged planning this wedding and still managed to look absolutely stunning today. Stand up, Susie—Susan. Just look at her!"

Susan stood, waving and smiling and wincing against the sun. She turned in a slow spin. Her skirt clung to her round breasts and round hips, lifting her flat ass. A guest whistled. A roofer followed suit. As Susan gave a half curtsy, the best man mouthed something to Michaela. She laughed and ducked her chin.

"That's enough, that's enough," Greg said. "No, don't sit down, Susie, not yet. Because I also want to thank my wife, Helen—that's right, honey, stand up." The guests cheered again, volume waning. "These two are the dream team, ladies and gentlemen. *These two*. Where would I be without them?" The two stood with a wide space between them. Helen accepted Susan's hand. "You know, people keep asking how hard it was to spend so much time planning together, us three. They just can't believe that with our history, there could be any love there. I've got to admit it—this question breaks my heart. As I mentioned this morning, there is a shortage of love in this world. If you need proof, turn on the news. Michaela's giving me her look. Don't worry, honey, I know you're stuck with sparkling cider. I won't dive into all that." He furrowed his brow and looked out over the tables. Helen feigned a cough. "Oh, I'm sorry, ladies. Please sit." The speakers echoed his deep breath. "What? No, I can't forget Helen's daughter, our happy DJ. She's having a great time even if she won't show it. Look at that. A real family affair.

"And, yes, I do have typed remarks—in my pocket. I used notes to speak to you as a minister, your officiant. Now, I'm speaking to you as the *father*. Of. The. Bride. The father of *a wife*. That requires some big vulnerability. Today, I'm blessed with an all-star marriage, but I haven't always found love easy. You all heard me say 'ex-wife'! I was convinced I'd found love when I married Susie. That's obvious—*no one* exchanges vows expecting to divorce. In this moment, mistakes and misunderstandings are the furthest things from Kayla and Jordan's minds. And that's beautiful—it's a beautiful day. But here's a bit of wisdom I fought to learn: Love. Takes. *Work.* It demands trust and listening and *forgiveness*. I know you both have some practice forgiving, and I'm so proud of how you've prioritized the future of your family. I know I'll never, *ever* take for granted the wealth of forgiveness offered me.

"But that's all just the groundwork. There's one last thing, and it's the most essential: Marriage demands *intimacy*. Emotional. Spiritual. And, yes, physical. But hear that *I don't put physical first*. In my first marriage, that was my whole focus. That's what our culture teaches young people, now more than ever. They're obsessed with *appearance* and *expression* and *pleasure* and who touched who, and how, and what's out of bounds. I don't pretend I'm exempt! When I was younger, I was selfish, maybe greedy—I'll confess to a few big mistakes. At that point, even if forgiveness was possible, I didn't know how to ask. I was cut off from any pure place."

He was walking through the tables now, his belt eye level with the guests. He stopped at a table of young adults and scanned their faces. Looked into each pair of eyes. His attention wandered, settling on the woman. She made her eyelids soft and heavy. She parted her lips.

Greg turned away, worked his words toward aunts and uncles. "So, *how did I learn?* I'll share one lesson. Any parent will tell you that your firstborn teaches you what love really is. Any father will tell you that raising a daughter turns your world upside down. Kayla was special—tender, caring, intuitive—a pure expression of a feminine soul. I saw that every day I was with her—which was never enough, honey, not even close—but there's one moment I'll never forget. It was long enough after the divorce that Michaela had met one of my special lady friends. And then, to put it delicately, the lady friend spent the night. I thought I was very careful. Specifically, *I thought I was quiet.* I was wrong."

"Oh shit," a groomsman said, too loudly. He slapped his hand over his mouth. "Sorry, Big G!" The guests were again laughing, and the roofers too, mouths stretched around bites of sandwich, rocking back toward the peak. Knees touched under tables. Feet roamed over ankles. The champagne flattened and warmed. The woman drank hers, the taste pear-bright and cloying. She watched Susan sneak a slurp from her plastic rim. Charlotte glowered, eyes glassy. She shook her head toward the high school friends.

"Big G—I like that. But we're getting riled up. Bear with me. I want you to picture little Michaela, eight or nine. Big baby-doll cheeks, fat gold curls. People used to ask me if I'd kidnapped JonBenét. Hey, I know it's a nasty joke, but I didn't come up with it. And I heard it more than once!

Susie is nodding her head. She can vouch for me. You can check for yourself—next time you go to the bathroom, take a look at little Michaela on the wall. Now travel back in time with me. Imagine how I felt when I went to check on my daughter at bedtime and heard *a man's voice* in her room. And then another one, really gruff, a smoker. And some lady on helium. Three strangers in there with my daughter, conducting a whole conversation! I was furious, terrified, ready to plead self-defense, sneaking up to catch the creeps when I looked through a crack in the door and saw Barbies and realized that Michaela was playing out some intricate make-believe scene. It was incredible. She had a whole script in her head, all these voices and characters. And I realized this was a climax—a wedding. I couldn't look away. Tuxedo Ken dipped Bridal Barbie into an old Hollywood kiss. Then suddenly, Tuxedo Ken ripped the velcro of Bridal Barbie's gown. Bridal Barbie was in her painted underwear, testing her hip's hinges. Before I knew it, plastic was clacking against plastic, and Ken's deep voice was moaning as he ground Barbie into the carpet. I was stunned. Sure, those of you with boys are thinking, *That's nothing. The things I've seen*—"

"That's why we knock!" someone shouted.

"Okay, very good," Greg stopped midstep, nodding. "That's one hard-learned lesson. Who knew that little girls played like that?"

A few people raised their hands. The bridesmaids joined in. Susan too. Helen held her brow, hunched and trembling, or stifling giggles. Michaela and Charlotte both hid their faces in their palms. The guests continued murmuring. Greg met the woman's eye again, too briefly, eyebrows lifting as he turned away. He cleared his throat. His incisors were sharp white.

"Okay, okay, we're all having some fun. But there's still one more lesson I hope you can take in. Listen, the moment ended quickly—not that I took that personally. Michaela was just a little girl—what did she know about sex? Don't answer that. I do think she knew one thing. Because at the end of her game, Ken and Barbie said, 'I love you.' Because when she climbed into bed, she left them cuddled under a blanket, holding each other close. She voiced their pillow talk from her bed, and maybe I'll admit I couldn't hear that so clearly, but her specific words aren't the point. Ask yourself what I'm saying here. You know why I shared this of all stories on this special day.

"My point is *intimacy*. To be held by and through and in another. Without that, our bodies would be as plastic and hollow as Ken's. True intimacy doesn't come from the body—it comes from the soul, and in her innocence, Kayla understood that. I can see that some of you are struggling with this. Yes, yes, enjoy the good humor, but then give yourself time to reflect and *permission to miss your innocence*. In this world, that's the real taboo, that's what causes anger and frustration. And there is anger in us—our base human selves. We're selfish and stubborn. I myself couldn't make sense of Kayla's moment of pure expression before I recommitted to my spiritual practice last year. And now—who would have guessed—I'm a minister! I can look back and declare that my daughter had it right from the start. Kayla, being your father made me a better man. I hope you make Jordan better, too. I hope you make *each other* better." He returned his hands to his heart, bowing his head. "All my love and prayers to you both."

Guests lifted their champagne. The bride's father kissed her round, blushing cheeks. He took his seat, straight shouldered and grinning. Helen patted his arm. Susan nodded. The roofers had returned to their shingles, bending so their low backs stretched bare.

Toasts went on: the groom's father, the maid of honor, the best man. Guests tugged at their bow ties, dabbed rivulets of sweat. They would cut the cake shortly, the hosts promised. Then everyone would dance inside. In the meantime, Jordan and his groomsmen pushed back their chairs. They herded across the lawn, to the garage's far corner, the high school friends leaping up to trail behind. The woman watched Michaela watch them go. The bride's face was blank. Her rhinestones blazed in the sun. The woman turned toward a click, toward Charlotte and the camera in her hand.

"You're still here," the girl said.

"Still awaiting my officers. You must have slow police."

The girl took another picture, closer. "I need proof you exist."

"Do you think you could dream me?"

Charlotte squinted. She dropped into a chair at the woman's side. Her bodice, though nipped at the waist, remained roomy enough to receive the camera and produce a small roll of bread. The woman smelled wheat and walnuts and a new musk, deeply herbal. Weed and ash. Hair crisping in the sun.

"I haven't slept." The white tips of her nails bit through the roll's crust. "My mom refuses to notice you. Has anyone noticed you? You freaked Jordan's friends out, I think. They're all smoking." She piled walnut chunks on a napkin. Waved her hand toward the family table. "I wonder if any of them are going to admit that they're mad."

The bride stood groom-less, an uncle kissing her temple. She raised her hands to her heart and mimed beating. Greg twisted to clink an aunt's cup. Helen and Susan leaned together over his back. Helen's brow furrowed. Susan whispered in her ear. A breeze passed, tasting of tar. The bride fluffed white tulle away from her belly. The cupcake-dress girl blew bubbles through a plastic wand. Her brother leapt to pop each with his tongue.

Charlotte snorted. "Did you see my mom's face when Greg got to the velcro? I bet you loved his whole toast."

"You weren't a fan."

"That's the guy that she chose." Charlotte flung away scraps of bread. "He never spied on my playtime. Guess I won't know what I learned."

She brought a chunk of walnut to her front teeth. The woman heard the meat's soft cracking. The mouth too dry, white coating the tongue. She pushed her wine alongside the breadcrumbs. The girl took the cup and gulped, coughing. Her lips left a cream film.

"Aren't you hungry?"

"Not yet," Charlotte said.

"Liar." The woman's voice dropped to velvet. "You sought my company. Tell me what you want."

"That's the second time you've said that. Will once more lift a curse?"

"Shall we find out?"

"Oh no, forest demon. I don't know where you came from."

The woman smiled with her teeth. "You're obsessed."

"You got someone's blood in my car."

"It was mine. I told you over and over."

"You lied. You mugged someone and dumped the evidence." Her hands flew up to the diamond earrings.

"Those things pinched." The woman's laugh was thin, melodic. "I can tell you a true story."

"Go ahead," Charlotte said, slumping, her shins sticking out from her dress. They were bone-thin and bruised. "Oh my god. Fine. I want to know about the blood on your hand."

"You know the little towns up the mountain?"

"You're so annoying."

"There's one with a little plaza by the park. It has a post office and a hardware store. A hair salon next to the grocery store next to the bars. You've passed through it. Last night, I stopped as the streetlights flickered on. I was thirsty. The first bar had some televisions set to basketball. Someone missed a shot. Someone yelled. Two men stepped onto the sidewalk, cursing. Each lit his own cigarette. As I passed, their eyes followed me."

"What did you do to them?"

"Nothing. How hurtful. Dear one, what have I done to you?"

Charlotte shrugged. She lifted walnut dust with the pad of her thumb.

"Pay attention. The smokers didn't strike my mood. The second bar had no windows. The floors were sticky with stale beer, the smell of molasses and peat. A couple kissed in a dim corner. A blonde girl tuned a guitar.

"I sat at the bar, thumbing nicks and water rings. I watched the bartender cross the room with a beer. Her shirt was sleeveless, her biceps wide with flesh and muscle, shoulder blades sharp under a wildflower tattoo. She wore her curls close to her skull, and the light caught her jawline. It glowed in her brown skin. She handed the pint to the musician, whose pink cheeks sparkled. She had glued rhinestones up the bone, to the eyes. From her stool, she conducted her words with plump fingers. The bartender nodded and nodded for a while. Her eyes drifted, her brows arching as she saw me waiting. She patted the musician's shoulder. And as she slid behind the bar, she fit a toothpick to the side of her mouth.

The musician played there once a month, she explained. And last month, they'd finally gone to bed. She twirled the pick with her tongue, leaning closer. I could count her freckles. I could see the bleed of her eyeliner, the chap on her bottom lip. I took her pick between my teeth and lifted. The wood was bloated, warm against my mouth's edges. Peppermint. Spit. 'She's a good kisser,' the bartender said. She pursed her lips at me, sloshed whiskey into two heavy glasses. 'But she won't let me take off her underwear. If I reach for them, she starts going down on me. Or, I should say, she tries. After the third night of this, she called me drunk, crying. Next week, she's having a surgeon cut off her labia. Then I can touch her any way I want.'

I said, 'Use the words she used.'

'*Trim. Shorten. Tidy.* She said she kissed me too early. She asked me not to react.'

'You looked up pictures.'

'From surgeons. Before, after, and botched.' She brought her lips closer, reclaimed the toothpick from mine. 'That's her business. Tonight, I planned to tell her we're over.'

'Except I showed up here.'

'Always on time to distract me. Go ahead. It's your turn.'

We drank and huddled closer. She always wanted a story. Her eyes brightened for terrible things, and for people like the historian, who seemed, at first, nothing new. An unmarried male professor, respected and cited and quiet in middle age. He scoured ancient texts from ancient Madauros and left little time to feel himself draining. Only at the end of each day did he know he was drained. And lonely. He made a diligent study of his longing. Tenderly, he laid down his documents and turned his keen eyes on his dolls.

There were thirty dolls now, four feet tall, or five maybe, depending on his supplies. Each began with the bags of lace, nylon, and ruffles, his ribbons and buttons sorted in drawers. Crates of wax and plaster. Supplies kept counted, stocked, and tidied. Measuring tape and scissors and plastic sheeting. Frilled socks and gold lockets, steel hooks and knit caps—better than wigs, which tangled and tore no matter how gently he brushed. He was dedicated to preservation. Such work began with precise tools.

No, each began with the template. It began at night, in the graveyard, where the historian crouched with his shovel and dug. He was not an archeologist, but he understood soil. The soil was cold under the moon. He was sure to get to the plots before their newly rolled turf and the burial lawn could. Yes, he had to move mourning flowers. Laid just days before, stems soaked in wet paper, the desperate pollen smell and the soil soft and moist under his hands as he bent to brush the last layer from the small coffin's smooth face. He opened it up. He found the dead girl.

He couldn't always be sure how they'd died, though he kept track of the papers, the obituaries and headstones for angels no more than one month embalmed, angels who *had lost their fights*. He couldn't do much with a base too stiff or decayed. Even less with one badly maimed. He wasn't drawn to blood and thus glad when he found the chemicals had been injected through the veins. More often, though, he found the incision stitched above the navel, the smell of formaldehyde, the organs filled. He found their faces already painted, hair smoothed, jaws wired. By whom? He studied each little feature's unique collapse, its sink and tilt. These chemicals wouldn't sustain them. He had so much to do.

The historian washed the doll gently. Warm water, a soft cloth, lather so gentle no skin would slough off in his hands. He swaddled the doll in a towel, laying her down on his workstation, the table large as a bed. He spread her legs. With his metal hook, he reached up into the doll's vagina. He removed each organ, aimed for whole. No need to saw or hammer. Only the cervix did not stay intact.

Through that same hole, he stuffed her empty torso with cloth. Then here was his best trick—a tiny music box, installed so carefully, resting between the ribs. This had taken practice. He listened to the tinkling bells and soaked linen in wax to wrap her limbs. He wrapped the head and neck, the torso. His failures with fingers caused him pain. He dressed her in gloves or a muff. He painted her face—peach chin, pink cheeks. Pasted wig and button eyes sewed. At the last, he dressed her in a lace dress and ribbon-hemmed stockings, maybe a fur-lined coat. When he set her on the love seat in his office, music played. A melody sweeter than words.

But before even the trip to the graveyard was the impulse. A vision sparked within him. He could see her exactly, so clear. He could see her in all her variations, with the frilled socks or thrift boots, ringlets or bonnets, red lips or no mouth at all. But only later did he see her with his eyes, on his love seat, all wrong. And still he would accept the company and ignore the drooping eyelash, the cheap felt hot-glued hat. Crooked buttons. The smell. Doused in perfume. Everything was wrong and then right, and time passed, and new dolls moved in, and old dolls stacked up in the garage. In the day, he considered ancient cities collapsing, the meaning of idols, the arrangement of rubble. He filled reams of white paper. And, after nightfall, he dug.

Ultimately, he fell to the smell, the reports from his neighbors, the astonished police. When the investigator asked *Why*, the professor searched for his work's template. He proposed it had begun with the girl-neighbor's funeral, the service he'd attended as a boy. In her coffin, she had been eleven, rosy, and whole. He only knew her from brief sightings at the market, running her fingers over produce stalls and talking to the farmer, making the farmer laugh even as she stole his grapes. Now the girl's hands lay gloved on her chest, and the girl's mother grasped his shoulder. Her tremors racked him to his marrow. She begged him to kiss the dead girl's white cheek. When he lowered his mouth to the stained lips, he felt the give of decay. The girl's eyes did not flutter open. She did not spit out any seeds, not bile, not even one puff of sound. Her mother snatched his hand. He pulled away and saw the gold band on his ring finger, the gold band on the girl's lace glove. Horror. He clenched a fist. His fingers throbbed, and he squeezed tighter. He felt the cold metal warm. Where had the rings come from? Does it matter? You either believe his account or—'

'I don't.'

'Detectives found no such ring in his collections. Perhaps he sold it. Swallowed it. Dipped it in amber—he forgets. He is no one's Bluebeard, never developed any interest in wives. The record shows he gathered cold dolls from the cold earth, and that only. He swears.'

The bartender smiled. She leaned close and whispered, 'Liar,' her breath a cool wisp past my ear. 'He's a liar. He fitted their cunts with tubes.'

A trio of young men had gathered down the bar. They were laughing together. Two held each other by the belt loop, their faces open and pale brown. The third man was shorter, his head bald and warm brown and level with their chests. The musician stretched a note, her lyrics muddied, her voice fixed toward the bar. The bartender served beers, saying something that made the men laugh together. On her stool, the musician blushed. The bartender didn't look her way. Not even as the voice cracked through a next lovelorn chord. She met my gaze, her eyes glinting. She snapped her hands clean of foam.

'In this one,' she said, sidling back to me, 'his toy starts out alive.' She spat her toothpick to the floor. 'I used to work at a dive far south of here, out in the desert. We were a tiny outpost, one of the only places to go. Which means we had our regulars. Some of the older folks loved to cycle through the same stories, especially when they could mark a brush with danger or a fleeting appearance on the news. One or two had been interviewed right there, at the bar, where they'd skirted rape and murder. They hadn't suspected it any more than they always suspected it. They'd kept their wits about them. They had listened to their good instincts. They had known something was wrong with that girl.

This girl didn't care too much about *pretty*, or else she did what she could to reject it for herself. She was a stringy white blonde with a massive motorcycle and a steady store of drugs. She only came by a few times, mind, but she wasn't easy to miss. So small and sneering. She walked with her shoulders. She slammed shots and straddled stools. She slurred *pussy*, spat *pussy*, let *pussy* roll on her tongue. You could guess the kind of things she'd be into. You could guess she would show you a time.

She often left with another woman, which didn't surprise anyone much. There were those who didn't like it, but few saw the use in making noise. Better for *those girls* to take *that* somewhere private. No, they couldn't always remember which girls, exactly, they saw go with the blonde. Lots of folks just passed through. Lots of *those types* of women went away. They lived risky lives, and their faces, their attitudes—boy. They passed through. Even the blonde drifted before long.

But when she was there, she bought the girls drinks. She had a way of touching their shoulders and stroking their wrists. When they played pool, she passed close, crotch to ass, palm to hip. She pressed her fingers against the green felt. She struck fast. With a two-by-four, sometimes. But only for those she brought home.

The bar regulars shouted the day she appeared on the news. Stringy hair and orange jumpsuit and silver cuffs. How long had it been, and still there she was, clear as day, walking under an audio track. The news called it her father's tape. Again and again, the networks played clips of the recording, the greeting that had played when his daughter's quarry woke, naked, shaking the haze from their heads. *Welcome, bitch. Look who's conscious. Are you feeling relaxed and rested? No, I'd bet you're all upset about waking up naked. Wrists and ankles chained tight.* His daughter's quarry, lured, delivered to the trailer under the tree behind his house. He'd saved for the trailer. Taken his time filling it to perfection, stocking the toy box of his dreams. *You're here for your holes and just old enough to know it. Young enough that the holes might start clean. Look at you, squirming. Big tits and no muscle, still tight and easy to train.* The centerpiece was the steel table with its steel stirrups. Then the mirror on the ceiling, double the open thighs, ankles spread. With the table in place, he stocked the trailer at his leisure—chains and clamps and smut mags and wire and cameras and baseball bats and leather whips and intravenous tubes and blades. *Old lesbians stay tight too, unless they play around with big dildos. I like playing around with big lesbians. I like keeping a cow pissing in the barn. If your pussy gapes open, that's a shame, but don't worry. I'll plug you up with those big dildos you're so sweet on. I'll take a knife to that thigh meat and dig.* He soundproofed the walls. Cabinets covered the windows and metal sheeting disguised the single door. Sometimes, there was a hot glare on his video camera, but he still made sure to film every new plaything. His daughter could angle the camera, zoom in closer. His daughter could take her bike out to the desert and dig another hidden plot. *So many bitches to choose from, and you're this month's selection. As for next month, we'll see. Not that you'll know when a day's starting or ending. When we make it go dark, don't scream. We can't hear you anyway. Unless we're in there, you don't exist.*

They played his videos in the courtroom, the news anchor said, but such images were too graphic to share. Instead, the news anchor described the images and played the recordings, with captions, an asterisk bleep for each curse. The news anchor, aghast, called the blonde girl an accomplice—his daughter—a shock. My regulars asked each other who had guessed, who could have known. How many girls had left on her motorcycle? And now here, on the TV, a survivor they recognized. She had been, allegedly, the blonde's friend. She alleged the blonde had drugged her. She'd never wanted to be strapped to that table. She'd woken up clothed, disoriented, but on her own front lawn, and soon, despite her bruises, she convinced herself the stirrups had been a dream. After all, now, she did dream them. The clamps and the tweezers and the voice and the smell of steel wire and, inescapable, her own fermenting self, her own odor enough to wake her, or if it caught her awake, send her heart pounding across her chest, because it did find her awake sometimes, this troubling piece of the dream. When finally a detective found her, she didn't understand. So he showed her her own body contorted on a small screen and thrashing, her calf and the shackle around her tattoo, around the swan, the swan on the TV and on her leg, which had been in the box, was still in the box, on the screen. Under the bag, could that be her face? The video gifted her a new static for dreaming—the relief of blurred shapes aligned with her wailing, the echo in her head. She hadn't wanted it. She had not wanted any of it. The blonde must have drugged her. She had climbed on the blonde's motorcycle, yes. Yes, she had been to her house. Could she repeat, for the jury, that she had been the blonde's friend? As the jury deliberated, musing over the ease of rebuking the tape now, years later, after a special invitation from police. How could they know she hadn't wanted it? How could a reasonable person know?

And when the *Guilty* at last came down through the media, the questions shot between regulars sounded much the same. The father would serve life; the blonde, two years. It wasn't enough—she hadn't noticed a whole torture workshop planted in her backyard? It was too much—what did she have to gain from any of it, especially spiking her own friend's beer? How could such a young girl make that choice? Small blonde, tiny on the back of her motorcycle. Porn and the things they see these days, what they see everywhere, poison, and the worst of them hunt it down, prowling, she was a wolf in a wig. A transfigured dragon, or a spotted snake. A bag of stones in a wig. If she'd been real, they would have smelled the mean on her. Hadn't they smelled the mean on her? And she saw their noses twitching in the air, their hackles raising, and *she sure knew to keep her distance*, and she hadn't really wanted it anyway, her heart wasn't in it—*she was reckless. She got lucky. She was lucky she didn't pick me.*'

The bartender bent closer, her eyes blazing. I watched the sweat bead on her lip.

She said, 'I know the blonde locked the women in there. She strapped them into that chair all by herself, and, yes, for him, just like he asked, just like she agreed. She stole their clothes and buried their shit and kissed them outside the bar before the motorcycle, before they lost control of their tongues. She tasted all that electricity. Is it better to believe that he forced her? That she wanted to? She doesn't appear in the videos. She locked the women in the box with her key.'

'Her father's key,' I said.

'Her copy.' She tapped the counter. 'She didn't hold them down because she wanted them. She tricked herself, maybe, sure—thought she was getting away with something, thought she was inventing anything, shouting *fuck the rules*, and I hate her. More than her father, more than your history man, and I'm tired of these kinds of stories. Finally, I'm tired. If I'm not careful, I might start to wonder if these assholes have something to do with me.'

'They wanted what they wanted and they took it.'

'Then poor me, wanting more than one thing.' The bartender nodded toward the musician. 'She tongued me like an envelope, like sealing a bill, and now she does owe me—I never wanted to know what they named all the surgeries. *The Barbie Procedure.* Every piece cut off and stitched flat, stapled down. And I looked at photographs. Before, after, during. I don't know what I expected to see.'

'Nothing you have to remember.'

I lifted my glass. She raised hers.

'Too late. Now it's mine.'

We drank, and she poured, and again, shaking out the burned sinus, esophagus, the crackle of the musician's last note. One of the young men clapped, and she winked her thanks. *With some help, I might sing something happier.* The air didn't move. The bartender cranked up a playlist, heavy drums. The musician's eyes watered as she traded her microphone for a stool at the bar, slouching, her joints open and round face warmed rosy, her pink tongue wetting her lips. This time, the bartender brought her vodka, soda, lime. *Lime? Are you mad at me?* The bartender denied this. They debated who had neglected whose texts through the day. *I'll slice a new lemon, then, just for you. No, no. No, no.* I was introduced as a friend. The musician petted her ankle, stretching the hole in her tights. She wore black, head to toe, and unasked, she explained this, the ease, the slim promise, *did she tell you I try to look cool? Did she tell you anything? Yes or no, both feel worse.* We did shots. I sucked lemon. They went quiet when they brushed hands. And my own hand isn't bloody yet, is it, even after all I've told. Pay attention—when the time comes for motion, it's simple—patterns of impulse and touch. Minutes passed. Likely hours. The musician pouted and drank—*next week, I tour the whole state*—and the couple in the corner slid ice cubes behind ears, down jaws. The short man kissed one tall man against a wall. Their third swayed on the dance floor, eyes closed and lips smiling around the insistent, airy synth.

I don't hate you, the bartender said. Once, three times. *Let's have fun. You leave soon.* We agreed to enjoy ourselves. When the bar at last emptied, the musician tried not to cry. *That call yesterday—I didn't.* The bartender calmed her. Everyone would feel better outside, where street and sidewalk now lay empty. The moon shone full. It rolled over the musician's rhinestones, the bartender's lifted chin. A moth flickered past, and the musician squealed, and the bartender lay a hand on her shoulder. I fell back to let them lead, walking close, murmuring. I smelled the calm dark, blooming jasmine. I followed down the path through the park.

We came to a playground. Swings and towers and bridges rose in tangled shadows. The musician burst into giggles and darted to the top of the slide. It was a plastic tube, squat and scuffed, its yellow almost opaque. Inside, her shadow slid slowly and stalled, reclining, angled. Her heels hung past the edge of the slide's curved tongue. *How cozy*, she called, or something like it. Leaves rustled overhead.

'I played in a park just like this,' said the bartender, 'though we had sand when I was a child. Tanbark, which smelled best after rainstorms.' She bounced on the rubber beside the slide's mouth.

The musician's voice echoed. 'Kids don't even get splinters. I remember when my park had a pervert. He showed his penis to a third-grade girl. My mom wouldn't let me play outside for months, so long I thought I was in trouble. If I want, I can still feel that tightness right at the join of my ribs.'

'You remember too well.'

'Always.' She pointed her toes in midair. 'I wish you'd admit that you're mad at me.'

'Why demand she say anything,' I knelt at the tongue of the slide, 'when you can hush.' But she cried out as I grasped her ankles. Bent her neck to peer down the dark tube. Trying to track the creep of my hands as they circled. Fingering the nylon hole at her tendon, the run up her shin. I felt the bartender's body behind me. Her stare fixed on my knuckles. Vibrations. The kneecap rippling heat.

'I'm ticklish.' The musician squirmed.

The bartender bent over us. 'Kick her away.'

'I can't.' Her knees locked, rigid.

'You're not even trying. I can't be the only one who tries.'

The musician gasped. The slide trembled. My fingers pried between her thick thighs, the thin tights and sweat there—are you listening? Staring from the shadows, crouched in the bushes. What do you see? The musician, writhing as instructed, and failing. The bartender floating up the slide's ladder. Her shadow above us, at the top of the tube, filling the halo of light.

'You look small in there.'

The musician's face lifts, straining to see her.

'We could have had fun together,' the bartender says.

'I want that,' whispers the musician.

I squeeze her inner thigh. 'You still could. There's something you owe her.'

Her thighs clamp around my fingers. 'Whatever it is—'

The bartender says, 'She can learn.'

'If she wants to. Do you want to?'

'I can,' the musician breathes. 'Yes.'

'Then you'll listen.'

'Turn over.'

'Onto your belly.'

'Just like that.'

The musician twists and settles. I look up the line of her back. And there is my hand cupping her ass and the bartender's legs floating into the slide, bare now, her knees and shins draping fast over shoulders, pinning shoulders as I finger the hem of warm tights. I find the slit sewn into the control top, the place nylon parts under the cunt. I stretch it open to reach stubble, ingrown hairs, satin underwear, aloe, ammonia, and rust.

Beneath the bartender, the musician's voice whistles. 'I can't move. I can't breathe.'

'Know her smell.' I watch the bartender's feet arch and flex. Her hips settle, lower. Her heels knead the musician's back. 'You've sunk your face here before and you've done a bad job of it, so let's see how you do looking up. She's lying back now, her low back arched up and outside, her eyes closed under the moon. She can't hear you anymore, pouring pictures in your hungry head. Who is dripping venom in your ear?'

I prod the musician's damp underwear. In the dark, the satin is soaked green, maybe blue. The cunt beneath is full and giving. An inner lobe peaks from the crotch's hemline. It falls loose, long through the slit of the tights.

I hiss, 'Here you are.' I stroke the lobe and feel it stretch. 'You don't exist to them, but you can feel this. What sweet nerves branch low here.' Her ass flexes round, and I rub it. In rhythm, I rub the left cheek and the lobe. 'She doesn't start open like you do. Feel my fingers. Kiss the tops of her thighs. Take your time, and when you feel moved to bite, do it gently. The tiniest pinch of skin between your two front teeth, and how slowly you close your lips. But you know how to kiss. You do.'

I sink my teeth in her ass. She shudders, almost kicks.

'Come now,' I said, knuckling the satin underwear sideways, peeling it back from her vulva, coaxing her long lobes to ripple down. 'None of that. Her naked cunt can feel the warm air. Feel the warm air on your mouth. On your tongue as you uncurl it. The tip of your tongue stretching to taste her. Like this.' I slide my finger along her labia. 'The tender inner wall. Lick there slowly, to savor. Listen to the wet sounds.' They echo around us, slick, lapping. The plastic ceiling collects sweat.

I graze her lobes' uneven edges. The outer stubble, the inner folds and ridges, tissue abundant under my thumb. I make scissors of my fingers. I seize a lobe, pinch and pull. 'You feel this,' I say. 'She feels the sides of your tongue. And that tip of that tongue, grazing her long, hard clit. Don't be bashful. Her clit, lounging right here in front of you. Kiss it now. Feel it thicken. Cradle it on your tongue.'

The bartender's ankles begin to tremor. My two fingers knead and glide.

'Ah, now here's that throbbing. From her clit through your mouth, through your pulse, down to my fingers between your thighs. Sync yourself to it. Run the tip of your tongue down her clit. Lick small circles now. Lovely. Doesn't she like a tight spiral. Focus now. You are your tongue, flickering. You reject the blood rushing to the folds in my hand. Don't lose focus. It doesn't matter what my hand starts to do, how it works to satisfy.' I follow a lobe to the clit, untuck its curling hood. 'You'll know you've done well when you taste jicama. The slightest sweet.'

My thumb meets the clit as my forefinger hooks backward. It passes through the vestibule of her cunt. The middle finger follows, crowding, center knuckles greeting the cunt's ridged wall. My hand twists so my fingers can stroke her clit from behind, finding where the nerves stretch and flex inside. I say, 'You think you're lying here still, but learn something: the cunt is a muscle. It softens and tenses. It kicks.'

I set my two fingers to pulsing. They expand and contract, nudging against close cunt walls. Space opens. A millimeter.

I feel her cervix, low and dilated. I feel the ends of thin wire strings. Her cunt seizes then, squeezing. My fingers tilt away from the strings, my wrist untwisting so my forearm scoops under her, so my fingertips hook toward her spine. Resting, pulsing. The two fingers make room for a third. A fourth. Four fingers, huddled tight in the cunt, in the clit.

The musician moans, and the bartender moans, and the plastic tube vibrates with them. Sweat coats my forehead. A drop of blood leaks to my palm. My four fingers spread open inside her. My four fingers close. Spread and close, spanning further, stretching. Her cunt opens wide. My thumb tucks to my palm, greeting hot blood. She thrusts her ass up and back. Again, she rocks back, her hips sinking as I close my fingers. The last knuckles slide inside.

My fingers rest there, long, filling her. The bartender's feet arch and I say, 'You can feel this. You can feel my hand ripping out all this tissue. I could tear the mess from the root.' My fingers curl forward, climbing, snagging the cervix. 'I wonder how deep it starts.'

I clench my fist inside her. There is always more room. She stops her breathing. I say, 'I could leave you scraped empty. But you're not sucking her clit.'

The bartender cries out, far above us. Her toes claw the ceiling of the slide, and the musician lifts her face, gasping as my hand plunges deep. Her cunt contracts. Her cunt closes around my knuckles and my knuckles open against her cunt, the tight lung of my fist expanding, deflating, expanding, deflating, rapping a regular pace. The smell of copper overtakes all others. Blood trickles down my wrist. Then the musician yelps. Her cunt seizes and her legs kick and liquid bursts over my forearm, sprays sour mist on my chest. Blood and cum swirl together, pooled on the slide's yellow tongue. I watched limbs droop above me, felt the cunt bear down on my fist. My hand uncurled, sinking down from her, fondling her lobes. She was quiet, and the bartender was quiet, and the park was quiet. I stood. I lifted my hand in the moonlight, stretching a wet web. My scabs were soft or gone. I touched the bartender's top lip. She smiled and lay still, and I left them both there dripping, limbs open, to follow the gray path back through the black trees. I didn't glance back. There was nothing left to see."

Charlotte sat hunched. She picked at her thumbnail, prying up the plastic edge.

"What then?" she mumbled.

"I walked. A girl came to me at a gas station. She invited me into her car. Touched, I accepted. Poor thing, all alone. She wanted company on the road. To feel safe."

Charlotte's lips were screwed tight. "You didn't say how you cut yourself."

"Oh dear." The woman wiggled her fingers. The sun showed each small, closed cut, dry and plain. "Is that the story you wanted? You should be more precise with your words."

"You're unbearable." Charlotte looked into her lap and then up again, past the woman to the sliding glass door. The caterer was there, walking backward, guiding the tall white cake. The doorframe tilted the cake toppers. Loose petals spackled icing on the lawn. Turning back, Charlotte sucked her cheeks hollow. She met the woman's eye.

"The cake looks disgusting."

"You're proud you're not hungry. You've absorbed your own lie."

"Wow, somehow period sex didn't fix my appetite." Finger down her throat, Charlotte gagged.

The woman grabbed Charlotte's arm, encircled the wristbone. "You're too thin to menstruate. And look how you tear at yourself. Is that all the pleasure you're after? The release of loosing your threads?"

Charlotte yanked away. "Don't touch me."

"There are other ways to unravel, Charlotte. How exhausting to stay whole and afraid."

"I don't want you to dissect me." Charlotte's eyes went red, watering.

"Again, always in negatives."

"I pretended you might be a little bit interesting. You're just someone else full of shit."

There was a cheer from the head table. Charlotte snapped to the sound. The woman watched a blue vein thump in her neck. She watched the bridal party reach for the groom as he walked toward them, his fingers pointed in guns.

"Jesus Christ," Charlotte muttered, her forehead sinking to her palm.

"Such relief—time to join them."

"No."

And she remained collapsing, her body curled away from the woman's seat. The soft brown hairs at her nape were matted by sweat. The groom blotted his forehead with his sleeve and approached the white cake. He put his bride's hand on the knife. The neat slice, the guests cheering, the photographs. She fingered frosting around his pink lips. He smeared the neat slice across her jaw, up her nostrils. Red jelly glazed her cheeks, and he kissed her, and her hands cupped to shield her bodice, all that tulle. The guests laughed and Greg laughed as he dangled a napkin. Michaela smiled as she wiped her chin.

The bride's mother, though, was already up and approaching, her stilettos hooked on her fingers, empty champagne flute at her hip. She tapped Charlotte's shoulder. *Find your mother in the house. She needs you. The day's not over. Let's go.* Chairs shifted, and bodies. Charlotte kept her back to the woman. She weaved away, around the caterer who, eyes averted, delivered two slabs of cake.

"We'll save her a piece," Susan said, sinking into Charlotte's seat, brushing at breadcrumbs. "Not that she'll eat it. She has more restraint than me." She slid a forkful into her mouth and then out, sucking. "Wow, this is dangerous. Don't leave me alone here—try it." She smiled. The woman chewed, tasting syrup, petroleum, beetles.

"Cherry filling. Divine."

"Strawberry," Susan said, scooping up some red jelly. She had a full face and soft chins, but her tongue was narrow. It curled. "Well, they got in the ballpark. How do you know Charlotte? You two seem so close, but I can't place you. Are you here on our side?"

"She's a charming little hostess. She made a point of chatting with me."

"Charlotte? Really?" Susan tilted her head. "How wonderful—and I'm so sorry if you've been neglected. I tried so hard to keep track of the guest list, so forgive me, but you must be on Jordan's side then?"

"I was his therapist, years ago."

Susan sat up straight, her chest lifting. Below her painted neck, her breasts were speckled with age spots, the skin finely creased.

"I think he hopes to be discreet," the woman continued.

Susan nodded. "I had no idea. And Michaela—why should she have told me? Not my business what he went through as a child. Or as a teen?"

"I'm sure I shouldn't say."

"I would never ask that! Poor guy! Isn't it awful how we keep our struggles—or problems, no?—all of emotion-goop stuffed down in this world? That's what's shameful here. He can't help whatever he went through." Susan lowered her voice. "Or whatever's in his genes?"

"I couldn't have said it better." The woman took another bite of cake. "Congratulations on your grandchild."

Susan beamed. "Oh, you darling, thank you! I'm so glad Michaela didn't try to keep it a secret. I keep forgetting it's not a secret—thank god times do change." Susan placed a hand over her rib cage and expelled a large breath. "Are you here with your husband? Or"—her pink mouth hung open—"a partner of some kind?"

The woman shrugged. "Divorced."

"Oh no, sweetheart, I'm so sorry." She scooted closer, smelling like candles, vanilla. Fine blonde hair tipped her ears. "It's rude of me to pry."

"She cheated one time too many."

"Oh, sweetheart." Susan's eyes welled.

"It's all right. There's no shame here, remember? Just as you said."

"We tried therapy. Greg and me. One session that he absolutely hated. He was right—it was useless, for us anyway. You must have heard his speech." Susan chortled. "You're off duty—I'm sorry. This is more drama than you need to hear."

"It's nice to talk to someone who can understand what you've been through." The woman squeezed her fingers. "Let me listen. I have room."

"It is nice. It is so nice, and you've been there. You'll get what I mean when I say that overall, I've moved on. Which I have, completely. But today..." Susan nodded a waiter to her empty cup. "Even without the wedding, it's a lot to be back in this house. You might not know I used to live here. Greg swore we'd have five kids. That's what I wanted, and he wanted. He was exactly the family man I'd always dreamed about. Masculine in that solid way. He took charge. He has those broad shoulders. He keeps himself in shape. He liked to say he was doing the work for me—why couldn't I do the same for him? I know lots of mothers keep their figures. He even said he liked me curvy, just as long as I looked like I cared. No one should have sex with someone they aren't attracted to. I believe that. I agree. But we were having sex, and I suppose that confused me, or I let myself believe we were fine. I didn't really think about it. I shut all of those feelings down, because we had a baby, and then suddenly, she was five years old, a big, grown girl starting school. Looking back, I admit I gave her all of my attention that last summer of freedom. The day I found out, we'd been out just the two of us, enjoying a movie matinee. Midafternoon, and Greg brought someone to the house. To this day, I swear we weren't early. No matter what he might say, I was always paying attention to the little details, to the time. I called out a hello as Michaela ran to her room. I heard the bathwater running—that always drove me crazy, how loud the pipes are in this house. But I adored baths. We'd just installed a corner tub in the master, a big one with amazing jets. It was brand new. So, when I got home that day, I thought he was pampering me. I would have called his love language acts of service—taking care of his girl.

"I walked up to my bedroom as the water stopped. The door was ajar. I heard splashing. Then voices. His and hers. Her voice was throaty and girlish—somehow both, like a starlet cartoon. He told her to lie back and calm down. I knelt by the crack of the door, a spy in my very own house. I can laugh at it now. I can see the whole scene. Me crouching in the hallway with popcorn in my teeth, staring at Greg's naked ass. He had a nice ass and that toned back. Effort. And the woman lay in the bathtub, under bubbles. I could see the crown of her skull in his hands.

"I watched him lift the ends of her hair over the lip of the tub. It was long, thin brown hair. So long it almost touched the floor. I looked between Greg's calves and could see the ends dripping. When I looked up, he was massaging her, washing her hair—I knew that amber shampoo and how his fingers moved so slowly, up and down. His back shifted, and I could see her forehead lifting as she rocked back into his palm. The tip of her nose was boiling pink, like her scalp. He always used too much hot water. He circled his thumbs behind her ears, and her throat made new, alarming noises, somehow breathy and thick. I felt them vibrate the base of my spine. I'd never heard another woman moaning before, not in real life. I thought, *Now she sounds just like me*. And at the same moment, *She sounds nothing like me at all*. And he was running his fingers through her hair again, combing lather down to split ends. There were strands shedding in his fingers. So much lost hair! His nails ripped down her scalp, and she must have been scalding if her whole head was that shade. I had a vision of his strong arms pushing her face into the water until it blistered. I

71

wanted to climb up the drain and drag her down. I'd never hurt anyone. The impulse passed. It was gone, and her voice was so rich in my skull, and his hands weren't on her head. I knew where they were, and I thought, *Stop, you'll cook her.* I remember that thought, because the next was, *Why would I care?* She took a long breath and held it. I leaned closer to the sound.

"That's how I nudged the door wide open. Helen leaped out of the bath like a shot. Like she was a ribbon of muscle. That one, she's always had those long thighs, long legs, and he wrapped one of our new towels tight around her. The screaming and yelling started up then. I hate to think what Michaela heard, not that she was old enough to understand. I didn't tell her about the foam on Helen's ankles, which I can still picture so clearly, so strange. She didn't shave her armpits. She dripped my shampoo all over the floor. That made me so angry. I made her bend down, right there, and mop up every bubble. I made her dig her own hair from the drain. Not that it really mattered—I found thin brown strands for weeks. In the grout. On the towels. One on my pillowcase."

Her words had slowed, her voice rippling. She exhaled.

"I sent her home with soap in her hair," she said. "Wasn't I mean?"

The woman stroked Susan's hands. They were swollen, her knuckles dry. "You found him with Helen."

"I didn't mean to name her."

"I could have guessed it."

"She's cut off all her hair."

"You both act like friends."

"We are. It's easier, isn't it? What's the point of sour grapes? That's all, what, sixteen years ago, and Helen really does try. I've been invading this house with this wedding, and she's been more generous than she ever needed to be. She's lovely." Susan looked down at their entwined fingers. "I won't lie though—I don't like her voice." She tittered. "But she's quiet by nature, and goodness, don't I talk too much. I couldn't stop myself. There's something about you—I know other women judge me—but you won't think I'm an idiot if I make her my friend?"

"Never."

Susan gave a small smile. She pulled her hands from the woman's. Laced them tight in her lap. The yard had grown empty and quiet. Gnats circled plates of frosting. Stray, sunburnt guests tottered toward the house. Two bridesmaids lingered at their table with their heads pressed together. One held up a smuggled cell phone, tapping the camera as the other kissed her cheek.

"I've learned that Helen's really an amazing artist," Susan said. "I'm sure she'll show you her paintings, if you ask."

"I will."

Music blared from the house, then snapped silent. Susan rose. She straightened her dress and licked her last drops of champagne.

"We'll miss the first dance," she said. She hiccupped. "I love the first dance."

They followed the pair of bridesmaids across the lawn. The music started up again, muddied by sliding glass. Susan waved her arms. She missed the beat. She hopped up the porch steps, and a run sped up her nylons, stretching under her skirt. A silvery voice purred through dining room speakers. Blades of grass stuck between the woman's toes. The other guests had also dragged chunks of sod. Pebbles and dirt on the hardwood. An aunt crouched down with a rag.

Below, in the living room, Jordan twirled Michaela through a spin. Guests pushed forward with cameras and sweat, fleshy biceps and freckles, clouds of sulfur and meat. Susan led with her elbows. Above, a new slideshow whirred to life. The guests ooh-ed. The infant bride in a kiddie pool. The infant groom in a pond. *Meant to Be*, read a cursive header. And there was Charlotte, hunched over a laptop, glowering at the crowd. The woman winked. She squeezed Susan's shoulder. Rubbed her soft, bare arm. *I put all their photos together,* Susan sighed. *Have you ever seen a prettier little thing?* Dancing, the bride's face was still round and rosy. Jordan dipped her. Her hairpins glittered. White frosting had dried in one eyebrow, crusted the rook of her ear. *Oh no,* Susan mouthed. She touched her own ear, shaped like her daughter's. Small and close, curved for sound.

*I*n the mansion on the mountain, the chimes sounded, and the cards came, and their people. Tidy cursive on tidy note cards. Tools arranged on a tray. The woman did what they wanted as they wanted. She was what they wanted. She was talented. Fantasies repeated in small and large strokes. Pleasures too. The women sometimes cried. They sometimes apologized for crying. Still, none complained. They'd asked for all they'd been given.

And then the woman's rooms were blue. Dark blue, fading purple toward the ceiling. Naked, the woman stretched in front of her vanity's mirror. She arched her spine left and right. She heard no chimes.

She circled the room. No chimes, no tray, no note. She picked through the tools on her vanity. Glass bottles and tiny gold pots and flat gold compacts and ruby studded tubes. A wooden jewelry box. An ivory hairbrush with pale bristles. She turned the brush over in her hands, feeling its weight. On its back, she found an ornately carved woman, her hair wild and long and woven with flowers, cascading around two round breasts. Her face was turned in profile, her eye distant and blank. The woman frowned. She flicked pale bristles over her palm.

Still, no chimes. She dropped the hairbrush and stood in front of the swan. She peered into its black eye.

"I'm bored," she said.

A moment passed. The woman prepared to repeat herself. And a note slid beneath her door.

"Clumsy," the woman said. She bent for the card and read it, then held it up to the swan's eye. She read the card again. The chime sounded.

"Okay."

The woman sat in front of her vanity. The cushioned stool was soft under her bare ass, against her bare legs. She looked in the mirror and ran the ivory brush through her hair. The bristles tugged at her scalp. They tickled the tops of her ears. She worked one tight knot down the length of her hair until it snapped away, ripping a few strands from the base of her skull. Then, she returned the brush to its place, teetering on its round breasts. She ruffled the crown of her head. Wisps fell along her jaw.

She opened the gold pots and gold compacts until she found a row of powders. Pearl and rose and dark gold. She coated her finger and smeared her eyelids in pearl. Traced rose along the crease of each socket. Blended gold from each lid's outer corner. Powder fell into her tear ducts, and her eyes watered. She coated her lashes in black mascara. They curled long.

When her eyelids were heavy with paint, she moved on. She placed buttons of cream on her cheeks and swirled them. Her pores tingled. She tapped gently under her eyes. Next, she buffed tinted foundation over her nose, her chin, her jaw. Powder flattened her face. She puckered her mouth and circled rouge at the crest of her cheekbones.

In the mirror, the woman parted her mouth. She twisted open a tube to paint her mouth coral. She puckered and smiled and frowned. Even in the room's blue light, her face looked dewy and flushed. Smooth and young. The room was cold. Her nipples pebbled. She rouged them, and they softened under her touch. She rouged her mound as well, through hair and lower, making her labia blush. The powder itched.

With red fingertips, she opened the wooden jewelry box. It played a light melody, copper gears like slow bells. The earrings inside were simple, one diamond teardrop dangling from a diamond circle. They pinched her earlobes. The necklace was more elaborate, a long, layered diamond collar. The latch was difficult. The stone settings scratched her breastbone. She sparkled as she stood.

The mirror was affixed to the vanity by a pair of brass bolts and screws. The woman twisted them loose. She lay the mirror flat, glass up, and kneeled, gripping the ivory hairbrush, swinging once and hammering down with enough force to split the center. Shards sprayed over her naked arms. Shielding her eyes, she swung again and again. Glass spread over the hardwood. Pieces bounced in the oval frame.

The woman again searched the surface of the vanity. She found three nested bowls under a scarf. She found a small bottle of glue, a small brush. The first she filled with the largest chunks of glass, wedges as wide as her palm. She found few of these. One, hooked like a talon, cleaved apart in her hands.

In the next bowl went the shards that could fit on her tongue.

In the third, she gathered the smallest pieces, the size of fingernails and smaller. Of these there were many. Slivers speckled the floor. Some she could only see with her nose hovering over the ground. She crouched on her bare hands and bare knees, necklace swaying, and collected glass in her palms. She flaked pieces from her skin into the bowl. She dug with tweezers. When the bowls were full, her fingertips and palms had stained the glass red.

The woman's bed was large and soft, positioned perpendicular under the painted swan. The woman carried the bowls, one at a time, to the mattress. She nestled each in the sheets. Then she stood and coated a swath of the ceiling in glue. The largest pieces of glass went first, one at a time, aluminum against plaster. She pressed firm and counted to thirty. Her fingertips bent white. Her shoulders ached. She created a long rectangle outlined by jagged edges.

Fresh glue in the gaps, then the second bowl, the smaller shards. She fit these where they fit. Her placements were haphazard and uneven. She left gaps. She counted to thirty. When she stopped to rest her arms, she sucked the blood from her nail beds. The glue was bitter at the sides of her mouth.

By the time she picked up the third bowl, the woman's armpits were damp with sweat. Her hands shook and stung. She looked up. The ceiling showed her face in bursts. Her eyes moved across the gaps in the glass, the pockmarks and fractures. Small movements shifted her features, drawing her mouth onto her forehead or cloning columns of eyes. She coated the glue brush in powdered glass. She filled what she could of the cracks.

When she was done, she lay on her bed, lengthening over her wrinkled sheets and under the shattered mirror. She looked up at her body strewn over a ceiling. She watched the flicking of her ankles, the curve of her waist, the indents at her hips. Flashing in the ceiling, her necklace exploded light. The woman fixed her eyes open. Again, she raised each finger to her mouth and sucked. The bleeding subsided. She ran her hands into her hair, stroking back, firm and slow over her scalp. She caressed her cheeks and her jaw. She traced the sides of her throat. Under the collar, her breasts rose and fell. She pinched her painted nipples with her fingertips and bent to meet them with her lips. Diamonds dug into her chin. She gave each areola a kiss. Leaning back, she sloped fingers down the basin between her ribs, over the fur of her belly. She squeezed at her hips and fondled the dimpled spread of her ass. Some of the shards above reflected only flesh, without bone or outline. These floating pieces writhed. They trembled and expanded and tightened and dissolved. The ceiling glowed indigo. Her body scattered over the mirrors. Her hands disappeared or her eyes disappeared or her feet. Her skin flushed and opened. She searched for her fingertips. She searched for the whole of her hand. She closed her thighs. And stood. She stood before the swan, squaring her shoulders. She stepped as close as she could, arcing up on her tiptoes, aligning pupil to pupil. Her face warped in the blank plastic dome. It seemed to wink.

"Who's there?" she asked.

No response.

"Who is this for?"

There was no second card. No noises at the door. The woman looked around her room. The canopy bed and the claw-foot bath and the shawls and silks and cream cushions, their embroidery restored to gold. She breathed in the smell of nothing. She walked to the door. It was, as she'd been promised—as she had promised—unlocked.

She stepped into a long, dark hallway. There were no windows. No open passages or turns. Just a sequence of doors, stretching onward, identical. One of them opened. A trio of cleaning women emerged.

One cried out. "We're coming to clean you up."

"Are you tired of your room? You can arrange for another," the second said.

"Any one you'd like!" the third cheered.

The woman shut her door behind her. "I have to pee."

The cleaning women laughed. "Impossible!" they giggled. The second was the first to grow serious.

"This means you wish to leave?"

"Yes," the woman said.

"Your cuts will heal slowly," the second droned.

The third's laugh rang bell-like. "And you'll never return."

The first pointed down the hall. "Walk for a long time, but not too long. Beneath a door, you'll see a strip of yellow light. That's the way back to the forest."

"The forest," repeated the second, "and the road. Good luck."

"There's no other place like this," said the third.

"It's been lovely," the woman said. "Don't work too hard."

And she walked down the long hallway. She walked and walked. She heard nothing from the rows of closed doors. All was quiet and calm and lovely, the long rugs clean and plush under her feet. She walked past many strips of light. Blue, orange, violet. She walked too far and felt it and turned back. There was the sliver of yellow. The door. Its handle was cool. She pushed.

The room within seemed an immense closet, spacious and spare, save the racks of clothing. Her jeans hung by the door. She fingered their denim hems, rigid waistband. She hadn't worn clothing for so long. She sorted through the racks until she found a loose cotton sundress. It smelled like mold and cigarettes. She strapped on the first pair of sandals that fit.

Outside the gates, the air was green and clear. Leaves rustled, and she smelled their veins. She sat on a stone bench, her back erect, her dress grazing pebbles and poppies, her diamond collar catching the day's fading light. The stone was hot beneath her thighs. There was stinging at her throat, across her fingers, the tickle of scabs pulling closed.

A car crunched its way up the gravel drive. The driver leaped from his seat. He held the back door open, bowing slightly, shouting, *Miss*. A bald circle shone on his head. She lifted her dress above her knees and slid over cream seats, breathing in leather oils and disinfectant and the astringent smoke of cologne. There was the rearview mirror and the driver's sun flap, the playing-card Virgin Mary affixed with a tack. Her wrists resting atop her round belly, palms sealed in prayer. She gazed down over the driver's seat and its seat cover, wooden beads knit together with plastic string. They squeaked as the driver buckled in. The woman leaned back. Oil greased her arms.

The car pulled away from the place and down the narrow highway, skirting the guardrails that marked the mountainside's sudden edges. Each would be a long drop. The woman rubbed the pads of her fingers against the pad of her thumb. She rolled balls of powder and pigment and skin. She cracked her window. Air rushed over her forehead, rich and tart, spores and minerals. She pressed powder against leather. She heard the car's child lock engage.

"I've got this anxiety about taking a turn so fast those back doors fly open." He spoke in a reedy tenor. "Better safe than sorry, right? That's what I always say. You don't realize it, but you're already having a pretty rare experience. You're a lucky lady today, and I'll tell you why: seventy, eighty percent of drivers absolutely refuse to go all the way up here. Not all of them are lazy either. Get this—they say the place gives them the creeps." She saw his eyes in the rearview. "Their loss. I'm all for you girls having a private place to do whatever you need to do. If you ask me, that's the sort of arrangement that shouldn't bother a soul."

The trees outside parted. The woman pressed her temple to the glass. Past the roadside spanned a wide basin. Across the valley rose another mountain ridge. Another thread of highway stitched through forest. Another car reflecting orange sun.

They rounded back beneath the trees, and the driver turned his head. He chuckled, bared his bottom teeth. "You're going to make me ask, huh? The things you ladies get up to."

"Was that a question?"

"I don't think you'd tell me anyway."

"No."

"Hey now, good for you. You've got a right to some mystery. If I was in your shoes, I wouldn't say too much neither. Some people are the givers, and some people are the takers, and the great big world turns round. That's the benefit of a face like yours though, isn't it? I bet folks want to tell you their whole life stories. Me, personally, I think some mystery makes people more interesting. You girls keep me guessing. I like to say I hope death is a woman; that way, it won't ever come for me."

He laughed at this. The woman closed her eyes. She leaned against her door.

"That was a joke at the end there," the driver said. "I can tell you're going to give me a challenge," he chuckled, "because here's my thing: I don't care how bad your day started out—nobody leaves my car without a smile." He patted his steering wheel. "That joke's an old standby. But hey, I could tell right away you'd be a tough one. There's a look people get when they've spent too long fooling around in the forest. Not that I don't appreciate some good time in nature, but the fact is, if you're not careful, you can forget how to have a conversation."

"You're refreshing my memory." She felt her skull rumble against the window, earrings batting her jaw.

"I mean it nicely."

"I'm hardly offended."

"Like I said, I'm all for female hideaways. You do what you want to do."

"How open-minded."

"The truth is, more of us should mind our own business. People need to let people be."

"You really know people, don't you." The woman straightened her neck, stretched her legs. "I bet you've been driving for a while."

"A decade. Rock solid."

The woman nodded. She slid to the center seat. "There's something I'm dying to know."

"Shoot."

"How many people have fucked in your car?"

"That's not exactly everyday conversation." He creased his eyebrows, condensing grease. "Hey, you'd better buckle up."

She stared back, unblinking. "Aren't we a pair, both so curious. You said it yourself—I always want to listen."

A moment passed. He met her gaze in the rearview and chuckled. "I guess I have to tell."

"Oh, I'm excited."

"And don't we all need a thrill. It's human nature. I've driven every type of person, and there's no kind that won't try to get up to something in the back. School kids, senior citizens—I mean, I try to mind my own business, I'll allow hugging and kissing, but I hit the brakes when things head toward a problem. And I mean hit the brakes—a good jolt and bumped teeth, and they get the hint."

"And no one has any fun."

"I have a great time. I mean, the looks on their faces. Who cares about a few tips? I only argue when they try not to pay. But you want to hear something fun? Are you sure? The fun ones move fast." He rolled his shoulders down his beads. "It must have been two, three years ago, I pick up this drunk couple, probably late twenties. They scream at each other on the sidewalk for a little, and then it starts to rain. The guy gets in. He tries to get me to drive away, but the girl throws herself through the door right before he slams it. They press up against the doors, as far away from each other as any passengers can get. I spot their rings, and it all makes more sense. I was married at the time, so I probably made some joke or tried to make them feel comfortable, like mentioning that my ex-wife was from Detroit, my little attempt to connect. Some people don't appreciate good intentions—now I know better—and either way, this couple pretended I wasn't there. Except, a few blocks along, the wife yells for me to stop. She says there's a girl trying to wave me down. I give the guy the what's-she-on look and remind her that I'm not exactly vacant. But she says there's plenty of space right between them.

"The guy shakes his head, throws his hand up, and says, 'Whatever,' so I circle back around to get the girl out of the rain. She's completely drenched. She looks a little younger than the couple, tan and tiny, and like the wife said, she fits right between them. She just has to hold her arms real tight against her sides and push her boobs out, not that she really had boobs. Her top is clinging to her, and even from the front I can see her, you know, her nipples. Realize, I'm only seeing these things at the stoplights. I'm keeping my eyes on the road, but at some point, I realize my mirror is tilted too far down or something, because I notice the wife starts plucking at the girl's soaked skirt. The fabric is clinging to her little thighs like a wet suit, and the wife is holding the hem in her fingers, cooing that it's such a shame. The girl nods and says she's devastated. It was her favorite skirt. The wife puts her hand on the girl's knee and says something like, *We'll wring that water out.*

And in the next second, the guy is bunching up the skirt. He's a big guy, so his shins are crammed up against the seat in front of him and his elbows are pretty much in the girl's lap. He squeezes big fistfuls of fabric and water starts running down the girl's legs and all over my seats. They've all stopped talking. It's the weirdest thing—no one is saying anything. The wife starts touching the girl's face. She tries to wipe all this makeup from the girl's cheeks, black and silver streaks right under her eyes. She licks her thumbs and rubs the girl's face pretty clean.

I've got the windshield wipers going, and they're making me tense, so I turn up the radio a little bit and find some nice soft rock and roll. I didn't explain this before, but the wife is really pretty. I practically gear up to tell her, but then she starts running her fingers through the girl's wet hair. She's wringing that out too. The girl closes her eyes real soft. I see that the guy has rolled the dress all the way up to her waist, and water is dripping between her thighs. And I guess I can admit that I tilt my mirror a little bit more. Her legs are sturdier than I would have guessed. Thin, but solid. She's not wearing tights or leggings or whatever, just these white panties that are soaked through. I can even see her bush through the fabric.

Traffic picks up, and it starts pouring—like sheets of water on the windshield. I have to turn my wipers up all the way to see anything on the road. We're ten minutes away from their destination, and I almost want to pull over and wait the worst of it out. But before I can make a decision, I hear something. More like a whistle than a squeak. I can see that the girl has her eyes all the way closed, and the wife is kissing her neck and her jaw. It's very slow kissing. The guy has two fingers in the girl's panties, and then the guy yanks her underwear down to her knees. He sticks his fingers inside of her, and I see his knuckles working like crazy.

I'm really about to say something then, but the girl pulls the wife's hand off her chest and moves it to her pussy, so the wife is rubbing at her while the guy moves his fingers inside her. Then, from what I can make out, the wife starts kissing her husband. Then they're all kissing. I can't really see their faces, but I hear their lips moving against each other. There's so much moaning. I'm watching the hands in the girl's wet lap. The guy has two fingers way in there. Enormous fingers. And I'm wondering how they fit and how that feels when I realize I've been idling at a green light for two solid minutes. People are honking at me, so I look straight ahead and keep driving, trying to figure out what to do. We're less than five minutes away from the address. The girl's hitting notes so high, I almost can't hear them. Then there's a yelp and a knee slams into my spine and I hear a crack—look right there, you can see they broke one of my beads. I'm getting cranky at this point. I pull over—barely on the corner of their block. I guess they can use a short, cold walk. By the time I look back again, they've pulled all their clothing back where it should be. No one says anything. The guy throws some cash in the passenger seat, and they all climb out the same door. The wife pushes on my headrest as she leaves, and I can smell pussy on her hands. There's a gigantic wet oval on the middle seat. And, get this, I can see *the tiny girl* walking five yards ahead, leading the way to a porch so close I can watch her lift a flowerpot for a key. She's leading them into her house. *Her* house! They follow her in holding hands, and right then I realize it was all just some game."

"And lucky you," the woman said, "invited to play."

"Exactly. Except, hey—all I did was drive."

"Drove and watched." The woman draped her arms over the neck of the passenger seat. She gazed down at the bulge along his thigh. "It's not like you could tell three adults what to do."

"Exactly."

"Not like you had your foot on the brakes."

"Like I said, it was raining. You begged for a story, and now here's the attack."

"Attack? No. Can't you tell that I'm curious? They have you pick them up outside their context. They don't ask, don't protest, don't react when you watch. Quite a bind for someone as careful as you."

"I don't care if they were cousins—it wasn't my place." He shook his head, gliding the car down a curve. "I swear, that last moment was the biggest, fattest letdown. Nothing kills a mystery like a damn hide-a-key."

She moved to the driver's headrest. She stroked the beads, smelled the glaze sealing the wood. "So why mention it?"

"It was there." He glanced over his shoulder. "Hey, you sit down. I promise that upholstery's new." His chuckle rose into a snort as a pickup truck roared up the mountain, its speed hammering through her window, down her side. "Goddamn maniac," he muttered. She flicked the stretch of seat belt above his left shoulder. "Hey. No joke, you're distracting me. Hey."

"Your massage beads make sense now. You're in charge and you're not and that's stressful, isn't it, treading there in between."

"I don't have one clue what that means."

The woman grabbed the seat belt and yanked. The nylon strap pulled, cinching his torso. The car swerved.

"Shit! What the fuck are you doing?"

She dipped her free hand into his lap, prying his lap band to reach the leather belt in his jeans. His brass belt buckle swung open against his thigh. He yelled again, words half garbled. *Off the fucking mountain. Please.* The woman's left hand yanked—harder—as her body sank in the back seat, lowered to her knees. She touched her nose to the wooden seat cover. She breathed in the scratched laminate, the sawdust condensed in each bead. Palmwood pulp. Stain.

"Then again, you don't have to choose where you're going or what happens there. None of that's up to you. So sure, sometimes, there's a letdown. Oh well. You keep those eyes on the road." Her free hand unbuttoned his jeans. "Not that you would have jumped at an offer to join them, those sneaky three. It's your job to keep driving until the bars close, though you have your own style and your own spots and, once it's late enough, the luxury of being picky. You take your time scoping out your last ride. You want to see two shadows out on the curb, and at least one has to stand." The second and third buttons held tight, so she swept her thumb inside the crotch strip of his jeans. She pushed and wriggled. "You flick on your service light when the standing shadow waves, ignoring how the other one crouches low. Better that she gets it all out on the sidewalk.

She's so tiny, and he can lift her to help her in. He pushes so tenderly, exactly like someone she might trust, or at least know, except she keeps asking him what his name is. He's big enough to lift her and he calls her 'sweetheart' and he speaks softly, promising to make her gag out the window. He gives an address, one not always unfamiliar, and off the three of you go."

The driver's cock had already lolled from his boxers, thick and squat, foreskin loose around the head. The woman spit on her hand. She maneuvered the seat belt and lifted the cock, folding, maneuvering. The driver cursed and swerved into the other lane. Branches scraped his window. They shed brown needles and dirt.

"As you drive, you see him rubbing his hands on her, her back and shoulders and somehow even her calves slumped across your backseat. She is a very small shadow. When you pull up to the place, he has to hold her up, practically drags her up the walk. He told you to keep so much change, but you pull out your cock before you even count the money. He cradles her on the porch. In the crook of his arm or over his shoulder. That's the only way to get his keys, which he needs to do, because she has started babbling some nonsense, mouth moving against his crisp shirt.

"After they shut the door and go inside, you take one lap around the block before you stop and park and kill your engine. You look for a light in a window, because if you're lucky, there will be one, and you'll have help guessing the size of the room. You are lucky. And, how perfect, there's a muted yellow glow on the second story, a wall perpendicular to the road, a window closed against a tree. The room a dim gray square and the girl hardly denting the guy's mattress, the mattress he has on the floor, maybe a box spring. The bedding is already tangled, already stained, sharp with crumbs. You see the girl's face against the grit, sweating vodka and whatever else was in that cup, while he pulls her tight jeans down so hard that her ankles flop off the bed and you can hear cartilage popping. If her shoes haven't already fallen off, he leaves them on. Then you get hard thinking about how dry she must be and how like the pad of a finger stroking a chalkboard and how he's going to have to work to make that pussy drool. Lube is cheating. A cunt has its instincts. It will do what it can against tearing. The warm dark around her stammers and grows warmer, more complete, and she is silent in the short time it takes to fade back as wet and still as he needs.

"You imagine that he's straightening up, standing over her with his cock out before he dives in. He rubs the stuff on his fingers over the head of his cock. Then his knees are on the floor and his hands on the mattress, planted at either side of her waist. She moans a little bit when he pushes it in her, but that's all. Her hands are limp at her sides, palms up, curled into bowls. Her nail polish is silver glitter. A real party slut."

The woman squeezed his cock harder. Slicked it up and down as foreskin pulled back. The car was speeding now, bouncing. "More," the driver whispered. "Harder." He thrust against her palm.

"Even though he's primed her, it's hard to fit his cock all the way in, especially when she's lying on her belly like she is. You imagine him slamming her cunt. You can feel the end of her inside of her. Those ridged walls. Her neck is twisted, her face bent to the side. With each thrust, her left cheek bone grinds against the bed. Her left eye smears liner into the bedsheet, and when he presses the back of her skull, false lashes wedge under her eyelid. In the morning, alone, jerking off to the lingering smells, he'll come into the blurry outline of her face."

The driver's cock stuck forward from his lap, tip bubbling. She massaged his balls. There was a smell of milk turning in its carton. He grasped his cock.

"No," the woman said, replacing his hand with hers. "Absolutely not. Because her cunt is decently wet but just lying there. Its inner ridges aren't squeezing. And he doesn't want to get his dumb slut pregnant. So he pulls out of her cunt and crams his cock into her little asshole. You feel this tearing. You feel the girl's eyes shoot open, flutter shut, turning off and away, and you're really getting close now. You clamp hard around your cock. You're sweating. On the sheets, her little palms twitch."

With her free hand, she moved the low band of his seat belt, holding it over his balls. The road widened, the trees thinned. She pumped his foreskin. She stretched the strap high.

"But they don't. Then you see the boy shuddering all of his stuff into her. He gives a good, quiet howl. When he pulls his cock out, it's coated in shit and blood. Still more things drip from the girl. You imagine her the next morning, waking, standing, rapt, another shuddering ache. You imagine the wad of what's left falling out. And you come."

The woman opened her hands. The seat belt snapped over his balls. Its edge dug into the base of his cock. Cum gushed between his thighs. He ground his teeth and whimpered, easing the car to a stop. She sank her thumbprint into his cooling spill. She dabbed sour to her wrists.

Outside, there were tall oaks. Streetlights. Evergreens. She watched the lamps flicker on, yellow light muffled by leaves. "I'll get out here."

The driver stared ahead, still and panting, his hands white on the wheel. She unclasped her diamond collar. It landed in his lap. He yelled. She unlocked her door.

"Don't look now, but I'm smiling," she said. She stepped from the idling car. No need to watch it sputter and speed off. She walked and walked and found the edge of a park. She passed the remains of a piñata—a round, pink ear, dangling at the end of a rope. Rainbow balloons deflated against a picnic table. Above them, a plastic banner: *Happy Birthday, Princess.*

The woman breathed the night air. There were too many smells to name. Teeming. She was hungry and thirsty. She needed to pee. She squatted, urine warming her ankles. Her stream pressed a pit in the ground, and the pit stayed there, herself leaching into soil. And now how the night bent around her, dark and quiet and new.

*G*uests danced close in the living room. They filled the pit with jerking limbs. The windows were closed, the blinds and the curtains, and time slipped forward. The ceiling was strung with round lights. Air-conditioning droned beneath the music's bass. Antifreeze and antiperspirant. Sagging bouquets, sloshing wine, and weed. Watching from the half wall, the woman felt a chill at her back and the heat from the dancers below. A tilted pelvis, sacrum grinding. Body spray and baby powder. Lilac satin, hips rolling, curved bellies, and panty lines. Pairs flashed together and parted, remembering where they were. Bridesmaids twirled bridesmaids in the corner. *You hate dresses, but you look so hot in them. Shut up. Michaela's lucky I love her, but I think I always look hot.* The aunts and uncles sitting upright, couches and chairs against walls. *Skip the garter then. That's fine. But now no one can catch the bouquet?* Pop song skipping to pop song, whispers over synth. *I think I know I don't want a boyfriend, but the second I go to a wedding, it's like, wow, guess I lied.*

The fathers had danced with their daughters, and the mothers had danced with their sons. Now, Greg did a shot with the groom. A tuxedoed toddler was handed to the bride. With the caterers gone, Helen paced between armrests, clearing frosting, plates, and napkins. She jumped when Greg circled her waist. Blushing, she wriggled away from him, nodding at the trash heaped in her hands. He turned to dance as she climbed to the kitchen. The woman stepped in her way.

"Excuse me!" Helen cried, her vowels nasal. "Oh, I'm so clumsy."

The woman widened her eyes. "Excuse *me*. I wasn't paying attention. Here, let me help you with that." She snatched up a napkin wadded around yellowed slime.

"You don't need to do that," Helen said. Plastic flutes and paper plates and petals littered the countertops. Glitter burrowed between tiles. She held a garbage bag open. "I'm sorry. Thank you. Right here."

The woman leaned on the kitchen island. Helen rinsed forks and cups in the sink. The music changed, and dancers shouted. Guests darted to the floor.

Helen cleared her throat. "Don't you like dancing?"

"I liked it when I was young."

"You're still young," Helen said, looking her over.

"Sure. But I've never heard this song."

"Not so young then." Helen's mouth twitched, her lips thin. "Can I get you something? I'm sorry—you've just missed Jordan's father. He's gone."

"You need helping hands," said the woman. She poured herself the last of some wine.

"You're a guest. My daughter will come help me soon... Though it seems she's decided to hide."

"She's an impressive young woman."

"That's kind of you." Her fingertips were red in the sink water. "Susan mentioned you're some kind of therapist."

"Every family has its tensions. I hope you're not too concerned."

"I'm—what? Did Susan say something?"

"Not her."

"Oh, Charlotte." She shook out her hands and took the woman's elbow, tucking their bodies by the fridge. A dark, sparse mustache grew at her mouth's corners. Strands of hair swept up the sides of her throat. "I should be relieved that she's opened up to someone. She was throwing such a fit earlier, about some other guest—god knows. She makes *herself* uncomfortable. Honestly? I told myself she'd make real friends once she went to college. She'd go on dates. Maybe even find a boyfriend. For all I know, maybe she has. I can never tell what goes on in her head."

"I hate this song," Greg bellowed, dancing toward them. He'd removed his jacket, rolled his sleeves to his elbows. He set down an empty cup. "Now don't tell me Charlotte snagged a boyfriend. What kind of guy could that be?" Helen's shoulders curled forward. The woman tilted her glass. Red wine leapt out, rushing down Helen's blue dress. All three cried out. There was a flurry of paper towels. *A full glass down the front of you. No, really, it's my fault.* The woman would help Helen fix this. She would soak her dress while she changed. She insisted. Leaving Greg open-palmed in the kitchen, they walked down the narrow hall.

The master bedroom sat across from Charlotte's. The paint on its walls was gray. White molding to match the white bedding, black-and-white photoprints in white frames. Books stood on one tall shelf, spines hidden, pages turned out crisp and beige.

"You really don't need to be missing the party," Helen said. She opened the twin doors of a closet. Canvases tipped to the floor.

The woman stepped close behind Helen's shoulder. She pulled the zipper down the back of her dress.

"Oh!" Helen cried.

"Your poor dress. I feel awful. And you were saying something, out there."

Helen's back tensed beneath her lace bra. "I don't remember. I'm sure it doesn't matter—I didn't—I'm sorry. This wedding." She brought her thumb between her eyebrows. "It's been a long month."

The woman bent down to lift up a canvas. A young girl looked over her peach shoulder, blue eyes drowsy, blonde lashes painted in fine oils. The next canvas captured the same posture, this head featureless. The third smiled. And a fourth, a fifth, backs and jawlines, variations of glancing behind.

"Susan thinks you're a wonderful painter."

"Oh. She's always very sweet." Helen flicked through her closet.

"Do these always hide here?"

"They're not finished. Even if that ever happens, they're not quite Greg's style."

The woman was silent. She sat on the bed, holding the painting of the blonde.

Helen continued, "These days, he's more…spiritual. He's trying it on. *Evolving*, as he calls it. Every year some new—no. It's not fair to complain."

"But you want to. In your own home, your own room. You're safe."

"What can I say now? The wedding's almost over, and it went as he wanted, and that's just the way these things go."

"Why is that?"

Helen pulled out another blue dress in dry cleaning plastic. She draped it over a chair. "To be honest, I think he feels empty. He saps each new thing dry, then he's bored. He—oh. You are a therapist, aren't you? Needling. Digging around."

"You need some support."

"You're a stranger."

"All the better to share with." The woman held up the canvas. "Tell me about her instead."

"I should paint over that canvas." She sat next to the woman, on the bed. The wine stain clung to the tiny roll of her belly, smelling of blackberries, sugared sun.

"She looks familiar."

"She's not."

The woman climbed to kneel on the mattress, her thighs behind Helen's back.

Helen said, "Not on purpose."

The woman pinched her shoulders and massaged.

"It's that—" Helen faltered. Reclined. "When I met Greg, he was trying on *artist*. I was—I did my best. We met in a community class, figure drawing. His ambitions leaned more toward the abstract, but he agreed he had to learn the rules to break them. He liked to say that and declare bold things, and—stupid now—I felt inspired. He liked to say that he worshipped the female form. Finally, he would answer the call to renew it! Reinvent it!" She snorted. "*As art compels us to.*"

The woman pressed her chin to Helen's temple. She smelled lemons and retinol. She stroked the vertebrae of her neck.

"I'm supposed to be getting changed," Helen said. She rolled into the touch.

"Learning the rules just means knowing them."

Her eyes fluttered. "I broke them too. We did. We went on long walks after class. There was a hotel room, but how that started… He was married. I knew, but he wanted to sketch my clavicle. Yes, I feel guilty. In my right mind—" A knot popped in her fascia. She sighed. "He'd get these flecks of paint on his calluses. I was swept up. My own husband had died—but no, I know, that doesn't matter. His wife knew there was nothing left between them, and she got desperate, modeled for the class as a surprise. Greg found out before it happened. He was furious. I didn't go. But I booked our hotel room and waited, not too long. When he burst in, he still had his art bag. He'd shoved his sketchbook in it roughly, still open. He stormed off to the shower. I looked. I couldn't help it. I thought maybe the pages would be scrawls or my cheekbones or blank. The drawings shocked me. He'd never sketched in real detail, not like that, ever before. She was in repose on the platform. I can still see the fold where her torso twisted, the way she lifted her right hip, that wide thigh crossed to the floor. Her body was familiar—I knew it. I knew it from thousands of paintings, women on chaise lounges and furs. I thought it was the most feminine thing I'd ever seen and the best he'd ever done. His lines move with intensity—I could feel, up her leg line, how deeply he'd etched the page. I imagined his grip, firm and light, the flex of his knuckles and his fingertips blending the charcoal, casting shadows below her rib cage so she seemed to breathe.

"It took me some time to notice what he hadn't drawn— her face. Though that was hardly a choice, not remarkable, not the point of drawing figures, bodies, the way limbs can fall in repose. He hadn't drawn her feet either, or her hands, and he's never been skilled at extremities, with their delicate structures and bones. He has the gift of other details. Breasts, full and heavy over her rib cage. The dip of her waist and how her stomach pooled on the platform and the low crescent scar over her womb. It was the only tight tissue on her, the only bit of charcoal that couldn't feel soft. I'd smudged his drawing without noticing. And there was something else."

The woman's hands were in Helen's hair now, working up the roots' oil. Stroked behind her ears, Helen shivered. Her voice lost its tinny edge.

"Was it real? I think it has to be, but it can't be. Greg had used one single colored pencil. Purple, between her legs. He was so careful with his shading, so precise, and sketching her there of all places, hairless and purple, like a birthmark, or a stain… Why that choice? That one invention? He'd taken such care with her likeness, or at least I thought so. It's not like I'd seen—or that I deserved to. I know I shouldn't have looked. I placed his notebook in his bag and waited, naked. When he fucked me, I didn't think of his wife.

"Later, though, the body reemerged, uninvited, and I was sure my memory was confused. My mind must have projected that purple the same way it began to fill in a face. I daydreamed a head on her neck. A heart-shaped chin. Pursed lips. Big round eyes looking down from the model's platform. When I pictured her, I always saw her standing up there. Her eyes never watered in the spotlights. She was pale, glowing, and she stood with her legs wide, and the artists gasped at the stain. Not her husband. She held his eye as he sneered. She heard the force of his blood pumping, his charcoal cracking as he captured her soft skin. I imagined feeling the lead point on my hips. Like every easel was for me. She would stare straight from every page, and she pitied me. She knew so much I didn't. Forget charcoal—she was an inkwell, a lake." Helen stopped short, gulped a breath. "It sounds foolish now. The expression I described can't be right. I don't remember the face, even when I try to. So much started to happen. Greg and I gave up paint. I'd forgotten. But these past months, it's been harder to sleep."

"Susan returned to the house."

"You're wrong." She slumped against the woman's dress. "These paintings aren't at all like his sketch. She's not her."

"You spun her around."

"The face isn't right yet—that's the problem. I can't find her without the face."

The woman's hands stilled. "Helen. I'm disappointed. So much time spent on poor work."

Helen stiffened. "Charlotte's looking for me."

The woman slid her hands down Helen's neck, past shoulder blades, under the shell of her dress to her waist.

"She knows you're a coward too."

"You don't know me," Helen said.

"But I know the body you invited. Don't deny what you did." The woman lined her fingers under the collarbone. She nipped the base of her neck, drinking in the round smell of brine. "You looked and you studied it because, mistress, she was something you wanted to keep. But you couldn't hold it, could you? You can't reconcile the vivid cunt. Purple, royal, what they called the stain of the slut. Did you only know your own pink, mistress? Imagine each woman pink and pale and sweet?" She unhooked the lace bra and fondled the red mark dug by its clasp. "And when you learned what you wanted, you retreated. Such a small, sad thing to do and to make yourself a creeping sneak for no reason. When did Greg find out you're a mouse?"

Helen whimpered. The woman dragged her thumbs down the spine. She jabbed beneath the ribs.

"When she knows it, her expression is different. Think back. She's not so hard to find. You can picture her better from all fours. No. Don't move. Remember. The tile cold under your knees. With your nose so low, did you smell the grout's mildew? Or is amber all you can breathe?"

Her thumbs dug higher, into kidneys. Her teeth skated Helen's neck.

"Yes," Helen croaked. "Yes."

"You still taste like it. You couldn't even manage to rinse yourself properly. Soap scummed and dried on your ankles. Mistress, you made such a mess. And she saw the truth of you, didn't she? She stepped on the edge of the towel and it fell from you like a skin. Mealworm, crawling. She daydreams your image too."

"She can't."

"You don't deserve it. You're already so low. Imagine her scorn when you confess to crawling under her skirt. You looked. You're not sleeping. You've shut your eyes to summon the color. You've lapped the juice from the plum."

She reached up and tugged a fistful of hair. Helen's neck wrenched back. Her cry was guttural, gravel.

"I shouldn't look." Her chest heaved.

"Then, when you tongue her, shut your eyes." The woman bit the notch of her throat. "I'm getting tired of this family, mistress. You already know Susan's face."

Helen blinked at the ceiling, her eyes gathering tears.

"You're a mess. Look at all of this wine, this sticky wet skin." She released Helen's hair and shoved her skull forward. She moved her lips against her ear. "Take a bath, Helen. Wash your hair. Pretend you ever feel clean."

Helen nodded. She held her dress to her breastbone and lowered herself to bony hands, stockinged knees. She crawled through the bathroom door.

The woman floated to the hallway. She looked to the shadows cast from the living room, the dancing thrum. There were still hours before evening. She felt the grease in her fingerprints. She rubbed the roots of her hair. Behind Charlotte's school portraits, the pipes began roaring. She pressed her cheek to the wall.

Someone close was gagging, retching. The woman tried a door. Fresh folded linens. She ran her hands on cool silken sheets. Then the next door, another bedroom, where Jordan sprawled on a white duvet, his tux rumpled, his head hanging over a bin. He coughed up pink chunks, yellow strands. Susan knelt beside him with a hand towel. He spit, and she dabbed his chin.

"There you are," said the woman.

"Don't worry," Susan cooed. "He's had too much cake."

Jordan rolled onto his belly and grunted. The air was rank with bile.

"I meant you."

"Is Michaela missing me? I was leaving the ladies' room and heard her poor boy in here heaving." She pointed to a wide splotch on her dress. "Obviously, I didn't get him over the bucket in time."

The woman crouched down. She patted Susan's thigh.

Susan dropped her voice to a whisper. "Michaela can't know yet. For a little while, it's still her day."

102

"There's glitter in his hair."

"Always playful." She wiped the bin's rim. "At least he's a good boy, passing out in his bed. I hope he hasn't left you disappointed."

The woman squeezed her knee. "Don't lie. You want me to shame him."

"What?"

"Never mind. Here, I'll watch him." She took the rag and stood, towing Susan upward. "You go take a long soak in your tub."

Susan smiled. "*My tub.* I heard the pipes, I thought… Oh, you're terrible."

"Yes, my darling, I am."

She thrust her out to the hall. She heard a door closing, the groom wheezing, a snort. She tossed the towel by his head.

Again, she surveyed the hallway. The groom, the cool sheets, the mothers, the locked bathroom, with its own muffled moans. And, not quite latched, Charlotte's door.

The girl sat in the leather desk chair, gnawing at one last plastic nail.

"Guess it's not you messing around in the bathroom," she said, swiveling. "What did you do with Susan?"

"Ah, so you do listen through the wall."

"That again. When will you get that I don't like them?"

Something cracked. Charlotte shed her last nail. The rest waited on the desk behind her, a pile of pink shells. She sprinkled them on the keyboard and pushed back its drawer.

"You've been busy." The woman walked along the wicker dresser, fingering baubles and creams. The camera. The diamond earrings, warm sterling. Golden hair sticks with pointed ends.

"I thought you might try something weird on my bed."

"You waited for me. Staged a photo shoot."

"No."

"Better to go for a drive."

Charlotte ripped a hangnail from her pinkie.

"No way."

The woman shook her head. "Aren't you tiresome. Don't you know there's nothing for you here?"

"That's why I left."

"Little girl, you haven't tried."

"Shut up. It's my mom who stayed. Not me." She sat up straight now, color rising. And with it, sharp citrus must.

"You drove all night to be here."

"After today, I'm gone."

"I know—you live in the dorms." The woman laughed. "But you sleep here. If you ever dreamed miles could empty you, now you learn that's a lie. Don't look aghast. Listen. As it stands, you've traded one white box for another, shared with somebody unknown. And there's fear at the first signs of that stranger, the book bag on that desk and the damp towel on that peg and, most startling, the gray curtain hanging around that bed.

"The curtain is closed, its fabric opaque. Who can tell if anyone's there? The girl is nervous. *Hello?* she calls. *Hi?* No one answers. No voice, no new face. Instead, the girl finds a bouquet on her desk and a whiteboard on the door and a scribbled note:

Hi! Welcome to <u>our</u> room! I hope you love the flowers and don't mind that I claimed a side, and I'm so sorry I'm not *there to hug you in person. I'm still scrambling all over the place, but I can't wait to live with you—I hope you understand!*

The girl studies her roommate's handwriting. She is charmed by each looping tail. The flowers are lovely but spoiling, and the curtain is strange but no threat. She hopes. She has not slept so close to another person since her mother and now imagines the stories they will whisper from their pillows and dreads the noises bodies make in the night. At least the curtain provides some privacy. She wants to touch it, feel just how thick. The fabric looks like velvet as the sun sets. She's waited hours. She's hungry. She squeezes in a whiteboard message of her own:

Gone to the dining hall! Find me there? Or I'll meet you soon!

The girl eats dinner alone that night, though in the morning, on the whiteboard, the roommate claims, *I was there too!* Idiot, failing to narrow the place, to leave a phone number, a description. What does she look like? She might have been anyone there. They will meet soon—that is certain. They will each give the other some shape.

But as the week and then the month unfold, it seems their hours can't align. Some mornings, the book bag is gone, and the towel is freshly damp, and the curtain hangs poorly sealed, so the girl knows there are moments when someone sleeps beside her in the dark. Someone slips by her bed and hears her unconscious breathing. Is it peaceful? Does she stir as the shadow floats past?

In the morning, she smiles at the new note left on the whiteboard or, sometimes, a stick figure cartoon. They take turns depicting misadventures—wandering into algebra instead of philosophy, losing a bra in the laundry room, drinking wine from the bag. They press sticky note stars on each other's study guides and hearts on borrowed books, hair ties, pens. The roommate is generous. She leaves gifts. A bar of dark chocolate, rich and dense with dried raspberry. A cashmere scarf in jewel green, *which feels like your most glamorous color!* A votive candle and batteries for its flame. *Will you leave the candle on if I'm out late? Or else I might trip into your bed!*

Except, the roommate is always out late. The girl falls asleep alone, and she knows it, staring as she does at the curtain, confirming again that that bed remains silent and still. If someone were there, she would know it. She would sense their presence, one way or another. She would be able to tell, she assures herself, especially when the moon fills and tree limbs dance on her walls. She tries to stay awake. She tests her eyes, squinting at the whiteboard, wondering how her roommate guessed green. She wonders how she looks sleeping. The lengths of limbs and how they fold, legs tucked or splayed, elbows overhead or hands curled under chin. Do they both hate the thin blue mattresses? Which wakes nursing which hip? It feels delicious to lie on her back like a frog, sole pressed to sole and knees open wide as the twin bed. That stretch in the sockets. She wonders what brings her roommate relief.

The thought of writing such questions makes her feel lonely, and she is lonelier still during dinners with two classmates, almost friends. They discuss theory packets and thesis statements. They debate who they will ask out and who they want to. Too often, they examine the sex they had in high school—sex which was, for the girl, always fine. Then she listens as the two describe fumbling dates, shrugging when it's her turn to share. They console her. They assure her she can have her pick of partners. And before the mood morphs to pity, they ask after her ghost.

One friend says, 'Your roommate must exist if she leaves you presents.'

The other says, 'Look for hair on her pillow.' They pet the green scarf.

The girl swallows. 'I think she's in the room right this moment. She asked for privacy. Until eight.'

The friends' eyes widen.

'I guess she does have a body.'

'I know she's having sex in your room.'

The girl laughs. Oblivious and obligated, she happily scribbled, *Sure thing!* She imagined her roommate buried in papers, not folded beneath someone else. But why should she mind? Crossing campus, she's sensed the desire lurking at each day's edges, the charge that passes cleanly between others. She's felt it leap past. But here it is, stalking closer. She finds her room alive with its smell.

She stands there, in the doorway, her finger stalled on the light switch, certain she's intruded, too soon. She wants to retreat. She wants to enter. The smell is hanging there, sparking yellow, and she gags on the toxic spill. She dreads what's waiting there. She flips the switch. She's alone.

At least, the curtain is drawn, the desk empty. The whiteboard reads, *Thank You*. The roommate has doodled hearts and XOs, and the girl wants to tear the velvet panel to the ground. It's her room. She'll look if she wants to. What does she want to see? Pubic hair on the bedspread? Noxious puddles? She already knows how the smell was made. The scene she's been left to deal with. She remembers the first

107

time on her back, thinking, *This is it. This is it. This is it?* But now she imagines the bodies braided together on the tight bed, hands clutching heaving shoulders, backs curved and arched, hip creases collecting rain. Does the flesh dip at the sacrum? How tall is the ghost creeping past? The girl flicks on the electric candle. She tucks herself in, hugs her arms to her chest. She watches the plastic wick, trying to map its quick pattern, wondering at which point someone said, *Close enough. That's the flame.*

In the morning, she reads the whiteboard. *Can I have the room at seven? I grabbed you a latte. I hope it's okay!* The girl lifts the cup. She tastes almond foam, cinnamon. It's exactly what she likes. How is it still warm? It's not right, she thinks. She wants home. She wants to stop herself writing, *Yes. I hope I see you.* And that night, there's the yellow smell and the answer: *Not yet.*

She confides in her friends and regrets it. At dinner, they search the roommate's name. Determined, they scroll through tiny pictures, endless feeds the girl has already sifted, dismissed.

One friend says, 'She can't be your friend if you never see her.'

The other taps her elbow. 'Even hating her might be hard.'

'You're not going to find her,' the girl says. 'She's not on social media.'

'That's suspicious.'

'Is she cheating on someone?'

'Maybe she shaved down her high school nose.'

'Or she's a criminal.'

'No—a Jane Doe.'

The girl tries to make sense of these options until she meets the changed smell of her room. What has it become? Anise?

Still abrasive, but not without warmth and, in fact, not unlike a fever and spoonfuls and a gentle hand on the brow. She hates this less. But there are smells and her appraisals of smells, and she is suspicious of both and adept at refuting conclusions, pushing instincts far from her mind. The whiteboard reads, *Are you mad at me?* and at once, the girl thinks *yes* and *no*. She writes, *How could I be? I hope you'll come talk to me.* She writes, *I can listen without looking.* She brushes her teeth and returns to an answer. *Don't push.* She erases it letter by letter. *I live alone,* she decides.

But every night, she flicks on the candle and faces the curtain. Every night, she lies awake in the smell. It is shifting. River rocks pressing moss down her belly. Raw egg whites coating hands. Apple cider vinegar and black mold and carrot peels, the sun on slate tiles, and blanched driftwood and opal, abalone, bodies swimming up bodies, and flour dusting elbows, steel grinding iron, and clementines, soaked chickpeas, the follicles of hair shed between stomachs, the curl tucked again behind the ear. When did she agree to all this, all these strangers sweating in her room? She can't study. Why think? The texture of the air always changing. The hours wandering, harried, stretching time before that last moment in the hallway, the coil tightening through her body, her whole self compelled through the door and the air waiting, whispering something new. The girl writes lists on the whiteboard. She ranks favorites. She crosses them out. How many strangers have learned her sleeping sounds? She wants them back. She wants to know how the roommate arranges the pillow, whether they both keep the door far from their heads. She wants to lace her last wisps of contentment into a veil. And still she feels regret when, before sunrise, the molecules start to steady. Some mornings, she refuses. She lies still, her limbs open, and slowly finds something flowing, a breath. She summons the river stones from blank air. Cold on her forehead and her mound, the moss curled with her hair, the mud weighing down her bones. There is a fog pulling her notice, but she's imagined the wrong things before, and always, interruptions, the steel saw, the eggs. She would rather her lone body on the bunk, pulling from her cunt a vine of berries and then the clear stream pool where she'll rinse them, where she'll float into nectar, and the more of this, the more she wants to see.

One friend says, 'She seems really selfish.'

The other crouches by the girl's chair. 'She gives presents to control you. It's actually pretty mean.'

'You deserve to know what you're dealing with.'

'You need to be safe.'

The next evening, the girl does not go to dinner. She does not leave her room. Seven comes. Eight. She fights her eyes open, dozing, jerks awake to pitch black and the lone candle's low, foolish light. In the dark, she floats and listens. She holds her belly and fills her lungs. Exhale. Inhale. Skin to hands. She parts her lips and joins the current. A sip of lichen. An echo as the curtain, too, exhales.

She picks up the candle. Inside now, a real flame. Holding it high, she tiptoes, grasps the edge of the curtain. She pulls the velvet away. And there, she beholds such beauty that the flame surges brighter. The wax melts. Oh! it drips. The girl follows to the skin and under it. She kisses her beloved's wound."

Charlotte stood. She walked to the woman, close enough to show the dust of dried hairspray, the white pustules on her chin.

She shoved past without touching. She opened the top

drawer and rummaged through socks. She lifted her car keys in the air.

"I want to go."

Her eyes were wide, shining. They flinched.

Footsteps stormed the hall.

"Charlotte," Greg yelled, "what was my one request for the playlist? I specifically—it's you."

Greg stopped short of the dresser. The three bodies formed a line in the room.

"You spilled wine on my wife."

"I also borrowed sweet Charlotte's pearls. Thank you again for the loan, dear." The woman unfastened the posts, and Charlotte seized them. She thrust them through her ears.

"You should clean those." Greg grimaced. He slapped his trousers. "I sent you at least fourteen songs. You know what, never mind. Where's your mother?"

Charlotte mumbled, "How should I know?"

"I'm at a loss. The groom is passed out, my wife is gone, the bride's mother is nowhere to be found. There was a line for the hall bathroom, and now it's out of toilet paper, and guests are starting to leave. Your mom should be with me, saying thank you, but my guess is she's locked herself in our bathroom *again*. Do you remember where she hides that key?"

The woman laid her hand on his forearm.

"This is my fault," she hummed. "Helen asked me not to tell you—she and Susan are trying to reconcile. I know. It's very emotional. What was it you said in your toast? Something about how forgiveness is possible when it springs from a pure, loving place."

"They finally heard me." Greg glanced at her fingers. She saw the rough pores on his cheeks.

"And they were so deeply touched. I said, *Don't tell me—tell each other.* So they hid in the master bathroom. They'll be reconciling for a while."

Charlotte's face puckered. The woman watched her eyes dim and glow.

Greg said, "This is beautiful."

Charlotte said, "Let me drive you home."

"You can't leave so soon! The fun guests are still dancing."

"Didn't you hear what I said? I want to go."

The woman said, "Oh, I heard you."

"And I want you to come."

"With you?" The woman tilted her head. "I've lost interest."

"Liar."

"Charlotte!" Greg said. "What's wrong with you?"

"She's all right. I can't say no to a good time." She rubbed his arm. "I make it sound like a curse."

Charlotte laughed. She laughed harder. She snatched up the diamond earrings and a fistful of underwear. She didn't look back as she slammed the door.

The woman waved. "Off you go." She tapped the camera. "Oh my. Look what she forgot."

"She'll be back in an hour. God, what is that stink?"

He stepped back from the woman and peered into the wicker hamper. Charlotte's sweatshirt still lay on the floor. The room was muggy, air vent silent. A square of light framed the blinds.

"I was just admiring your ministry license. It looks fresh."

"Does it?" He blinked. "I'm still new at this, officially—"

"But it doesn't feel like that?"

"Not at all." Greg sat on the bed. His looked her up and down. "I'll confess, I noticed you earlier. Well before the mishap with the wine."

"I'm aware."

"Who are you, again?"

The woman stood closer, her stance open. "Don't say you don't recognize me. Here. Take a closer look."

She watched Greg's pupils dilate. She watched him claw at his tie.

"This room is a compost heap."

"Here, let me help you cool down."

The woman unknotted his tie, working slowly. She dragged it from his collar. It was purple silk, unembroidered. She hooked it around her own neck.

"Whoever you are, you have nice hands," Greg said, reclining, watching her kneel to his shoelaces. "Feminine. Are you married? You must be. I can guess what your husband's like."

"I'm not married." She slung one shoelace over her shoulder.

"That's still a hint. You're making this fun for me. Are you one of Susan's friends?"

"No." There was polish and grass on his shoes.

"Good. Then you haven't heard too much bad stuff about me."

"You think yourself a bad guy?"

"I have my fair share of sins I'm not too proud of. The truth is, I'm starting to think, at some point, you learn so much about how life goes that there's a goodness you can't get back."

He wiggled his toes in his socks and stretched out over the quilt's white daisies. His legs were too long. His feet poked through the frame.

"*Permission to miss your own innocence.*"

"Yes." Greg's grin broke crooked. "You listened too."

"I hung on every word. Is that feminine, listening?"

"I'd say so. Absolutely."

"I've heard that before." She stroked the crest of his nose. Petted his eyebrows. "What do you hear?"

He hesitated. "Music." He closed his eyes. "Bridesmaids dancing. They're so young."

She held his left hand, gently, and lifted it. She held his wrist to the iron bed.

"Wait," he said. His right hand reached back, and she grabbed it. Wrist to wrist. She wrapped them in silk. She knotted the tie to the frame.

His eyes were wild. "Did Mariah send you?"

"If I were a better comfort, I would say *sure*."

His feet kicked, but the bedframe fettered him. She sat on his shins. Circled the first ankle with his shoelace. Tethered the ankle to iron.

"This tie is going to slide apart. Whatever you're trying, this tie is going to rip."

"If you keep rocking the bed, I'm going to cut off your foot's circulation." She pulled tighter. "That's not preferred." The next ankle went quicker. "Not to mention, the whole house will hear you. Your son-in-law's asleep right next door! I'm sure your daughter will search him out soon enough." She stood, watching him lock his knees. "If you keep yelping, she might take a peek."

A vein spasmed under his left eye. Lines deepened around his mouth, to his chin.

"Tell Mariah she's a bitch."

"Uh-oh. I'll speak more clearly. I don't know who that is."

The woman surveyed the white wicker dresser. She picked out baby blue lotion, then a grayed crew sock, heel worn through. She laid the bottle on his stomach. Packed the sock in his mouth.

"What a treat," she said as he struggled. "So many people come find me and then put up quite the fight. Though I suppose the protests can be part of it." She gave a dulcet sigh. "It's as though some of my guests don't trust me. Their little words interrupt the nice sounds." She undid his belt, his zipper. She pulled his pants around his ankles, then his briefs. "That didn't happen where I last worked." His cock flopped over his balls, six straight inches. He was circumcised. She lifted the pink head. He groaned.

She smiled, prodding his cock's slit. The urethra was tight and clean. "You wear deodorant around your ball sack. Cedar. Aluminum. Clove. And our lotion here claims to smell like cotton candy." She opened the bottle. "Oh no. I don't think these go so well together. And you have to breathe through your nose." She squeezed pale blue onto his pubic hair. "Good thing we like to explore."

She rubbed him, mixing a putrid sweetness. Aspartame. Rancid paint. Her hands tingled. His fingers went slack.

"I worked in a place built for pleasure. There were instructions. Each woman arrived with a concise card of her own. Short and strict, individual, certain. I was not to ask for additional insight, nor were they to provide it. They could not change their minds. Of course, I have excellent instincts, and certain situations became difficult. Still, I always kept each to her plan." She slopped lotion up his soft shaft. "Bite down." Lotion clogged his slit line. A wail drowned in his throat.

Humming nonsense, the woman swayed to the dresser. She twirled a hair stick and watched its blunt end's white rhinestone. Along its length, it tapered thinner, sharper. She pressed her thumb to its point.

Greg's eyes were wide. She brought the hair stick closer. "Do you think this is real gold? It has a nice weight to it, but that doesn't mean it's not gilded. Later, you'll know if it peeled." She coated the stick in lotion, letting globs fall to the carpet. "Mess never lasted at the mansion. The women kept it even cleaner than your home. This house is gleaming, but you can still catch an infection. All your messes still build over time."

The stick coated, she climbed onto the mattress. She gagged. She knelt on his thighs.

"Don't mistake me—I had a lovely time there. I'm lucky to know when to leave." She wobbled his cock. "Oh, we're slippery. Don't worry—I learned this move from porn. Not at the mansion, no, ingénue. Outside our rooms, we women couldn't watch each other. But I know there was someone else."

She gripped his cock straight. "There. In other circumstances, I might ask your opinion on watching." She stared at his red face, his nose pointed to the ceiling. "Myself, I don't love eyes on me." She hovered the stick over the slit, the sharp tip aligned to the hole. "This will sting. Look."

She pushed slowly. His jaw dropped to his breastbone. The blood vessels in his eyes strained. A little pressure. The gold point slid in the hole.

"I wouldn't flail." She shifted her weight to her knees. "Oh, listen to that high whine. I can feel that through my marrow, Greg."

The gold stick slid further in. One millimeter. The second. The tip shuddered open with each push. Greg held very still, wheezing, his forehead beading with sweat. Under the layer of lotion, the tip of his cock turned red. Half an inch. Three-quarters. Her scabs were burning. His thighs trembled beneath her knees.

"What a breeze," the woman said. "Such a straight cock. If you were curved, I would have forced it. I take back what

I said. Forget the porn. Suddenly, I'm sure this is a set of motions I've always known." Her throat filled. She coughed, savoring. "Can you find that smell seeping out of you? You've added cottage cheese."

Greg's breath hitched.

"You look pale. Inhale with me. One, two, three." She pushed. The stick plunged deeper. "Are we dizzy? It's true, the urethra is not meant to stretch. We're a creative species—cock doctors extract all sorts of things. Batteries, drill bits, a jump rope. A pencil, a pencil lead, splinters. A mascara brush. A pearl necklace—a nice little joke, that one. And my favorite: the head of a snake.

"Imagining the process is too wonderful. Did he find it dead? I don't think so. I think he killed it, and I wonder what started the hunt. Some youthful upset? Delight? Envy of swift species? He may have regretted the small, slick body dangling in his fist—the sagging tongue. Or he felt triumphant. No need to fear the hungers the snake might speak.

"That's what we predict. As though he hadn't already heard it. As though it wasn't the serpent's message that propelled the serpent's head. He stretched himself to take the tongue, the snout, up to the eyeballs and then—where's the end? The story goes, there was a miracle. He felt the snake alive, slithering in. He tugged the tail back, but that head would not come out. The dead snake dangled out of him. He grew desperate. He held the skull safe in his cock and severed the rest. Before he could stop it, the head, freed, disappeared in the body, where it has been swimming since, leaking venom, forever pursuing its tail."

Four inches now. Halfway. Fumes dizzied the room as the stick grew thicker. The rhinestone end holding straight. Greg's cock stiffened. She felt resistance. She felt him watching as she pushed hard.

"I've put myself in this position," the woman said. Hot lotion oozed down his cock. "Perhaps I'll go back to the mansion. If I miss it. I don't know yet. I don't remember what yearning first brought me there. I imagine I wasn't always bothered by the cameras. I imagine I was happy to take the notes, trusting the women wrote them. Only the scripts out here bothered me."

His cock was straining upright. His groan vibrated to her toes.

"Oh well. There's no knowing backward, so why waste the air. Are you breathing?" She smiled. "Good. No point in spinning circles. I focus on what I enjoy."

The stick stopped. His urethra was a pit in his cock, a plugged hole. She fingered his perineum and felt the sharp point. There was no deeper to go. She loosened his tie, freeing one wrist. She plucked up his hand by the thumb. Closed his fingers around his taut cock.

"Hold tight or there will be scraping."

She wrested the sock from his teeth. He whimpered. Between broken capillaries, his pupils were dark hollows, voids.

He rasped, "What did you do to me?"

"How do you feel?"

"Humiliated."

"No. How do you feel?"

Greg's skull dropped to Charlotte's pillow. His fingers pulsed around his cock, light, dripping lotion.

"There's burning. I don't know, it's hard to talk, I—" His chest heaved. "I feel full."

She stared down at his big shoulders on the twin mattress. His long legs, his white socks, ankles bound.

"Someone will find you eventually. You'll have to hold yourself together for now."

She lifted up the girl's abandoned camera. She took one photo. Another. A flash. He whined after her as she left him, closing the door as she went. In the hall, the pipes were running. She heard rumbling through the walls and the music end to end of it. Retching. Giggles. Moans.

Guests danced in the living room. No hosts, no shimmering bride. Only white walls and churning shadows. She mixed the girl's camera with the others. She watched a bridesmaid stumble. Watched an aunt cup an uncle's ass.

She could stand above this dim, flailing cluster. Soften her gaze and wait for them to draw toward her, keening, offering their lonely cheeks. But better now to walk elsewhere. Wandering, she would find sprawling undergrowth. Brambles, ample flesh, eager soil.

ACKNOWLEDGMENTS

This book could not exist without the tireless guidance and support of Jeffrey DeShell and Elisabeth Sheffield. Thank you for believing in this project through all of its fragments and drafts. I am also grateful to Kelly Hurley, Stephen Graham Jones, and Marcia Douglas, who offered valuable feedback on those sections workshopped in her class. Deepest gratitude to all of my MFA cohort and the faculty at the University of Colorado at Boulder. Thank you for your generous, challenging feedback and your brilliant, courageous work.

Thank you to the board of Fiction Collective Two for allowing this book to become what it wanted to be. To Sarah Blackman, who believed in this project enough to offer her time and guidance as it evolved into its final draft. To Joanna Ruocco, who has been supportive at every step. And to everyone at the University of Alabama Press, especially Dan Waterman, for taking me through each last step.

Thank you to the Writers Grotto and the Ruby for providing the time and space to think, listen, and write—and for helping me see all the different ways to build a writer's life.

For their patience, curiosity, and enthusiasm, I am grateful to my friends, from those who have championed my writing since childhood to my library coworkers and creative communities in Boston, Portland, Boulder, and the Bay Area.

Boundless love and gratitude to my parents and family.

And, finally, to Matt, who never let me give up.